The Finest Cotton

Also by Faye Green

The Boy on the Wall

Dicey

Gertie

A Daughter is Given

The Hungry Piper

The Irish Woman

Close to Home

About the Author

FAYE GREEN presents her 8th book, THE FINEST COTTON, a humorous look at aging. She has intentionally written a book that looks gently on this human condition while allowing the reader to engage without modifying or amending their views on this very personal subject. THE FINEST COTTON explores a universal theme—As time passes does the mirror reflect who you are, who you've become or who you have always been?

Faye Green retired from the Prince Georges County (MD) School System and the Department of Defense. She is originally from Laurel, Maryland—the setting for this story. She now lives in Milford, Delaware with her husband. Besides writing, she enjoys gardening, traveling and keeping up with her family in Delaware, Maryland, South Carolina, California, New York and New Zealand.

The countless hours perfecting a manuscript and getting it ready for publishing are worth it when readers immerse themselves in the pages of THE FINEST COTTON and ask for the next book.

Ms Green hopes the readers find joy in THE FINEST COTTON, appreciating the simple pleasure of a well-told story.

The Finest Cotton

Faye Green

ISBN 978-1-62806-448-3 (print | paperback)
ISBN 978-1-62806-449-0 (print | hardback)
ISBN 978-1-62806-450-6 (ebook)

Library of Congress Control Number 2025907739

Published by Salt Water Media
29 Broad Street, Suite 104
Berlin, MD 21811
www.saltwatermedia.com

Cover artwork by Hannah C. Browning; cat used via unsplash.com user
Taylor Deas Melesh; frame and t-shirts via istockphoto.com

Dedicated to

My Cast of Characters

Greg (Sylva)
Billy
Tina (Henry)
Dianna (Poojitha)
Julie (Tiziano)

The Finest Cotton

Mostly 1987
Laurel, Maryland

Cast of Characters:

Lucille Cotton (Grandma)
Irving Cotton (deceased)
Patrick Cotton only son (deceased)
Joanne Cotton daughter-in-law (deceased)

Sarah	Granddaughter -oldest
John	Grandson
Mark	Grandson (Pam)
Pete (twin)	Grandson (Sylvia)
Matt (twin)	Grandson
Jim	Grandson (Marge)
Regina	Granddaughter
Margaret	Granddaughter - youngest
Snow White	The cat

Chapter 1

Sarah, Mark, Jim, Pete, Matt, Margaret

S arah held the door as her sister and brothers filed into her kitchen. They came in and began talking at once. Matt, Pete, Margaret, Mark, and Jim. Some felt this was a waste of time; some that they had all the answers. And some did not give a *rat's ass* about this latest hullabaloo. Everyone came today except John, who never came to family meetings, and Regina, who was in Africa.

Sarah had called many Cotton family meetings. The last memorable one occurred when their mother and father died in a plane crash. There have been meetings called about graduations and pending weddings. This was the first one Sarah called about Grandma.

Most of her siblings lived in and around Laurel, Maryland. Sarah lived right inside the town limits, and the rest lived across the Patuxent River, which flows past the town. Regina always tried to live at least one continent away. As usual, this family meeting was at Sarah's house.

"Snacks on the counter. Help yourselves to drinks." Sarah sat at the kitchen table with Jim and Mark. Her organized notes stacked in front of her. Margaret was at the counter on a stool while Pete and Matt chose to stand. Sarah had three kinds of fresh baked cookies on the table—plus coffee and iced tea for her siblings. Mark picked a seat closest to the cookies. Grandma was not invited.

Jim opened. "OK, Sarah. You called this so-called meeting. Are we pickin' cotton today?"

Cotton Picking was the family round-table tradition started about the time the older grandchildren came into puberty. Irving Cotton, Grandpa, the patriarch, thought it would be good to give the grandchildren a voice at gatherings, including the oldest at 14 and the youngest, three. He set the rules: Talk about yourself, your opinions, or your defense (if some family member mentions your name). Keep it short. Later, that rule was changed to include a direct question to another family member. After the children began marrying, he made a new rule to exclude in-laws. No doubt the *Cotton Picking* exercise kept what would have been a dysfunctional family functioning. *Cotton Pickings* took place at the dining table. Nothing could be said out of turn except a small squeal and raised forefinger to imitate a cut by a sharp prick from a cotton boll. (None in this family had ever really picked cotton) Grandpa was gone now, and it was not clear who would bang the fork against the water glass to bring calm when things got out of hand.

"No, we are not picking cotton today. I told you, it's about Grandma." Sarah tried to get started.

"What's going on with Grandma?" Pete was always short on time and ready to get to the point and his golf club.

"Grandma went up on a trapeze!" Sarah announced. Mark stopped chewing his cookie.

"On the trapeze!" Sarah repeated.

"There was a net," Sarah added quickly. "The circus is in town," she reminded. It was true. The circus was in town, and they never let amateurs go up on the trapeze without a net.

"You must be kidding," Matt took interest.

"Grandma?" Pete questioned again.

"Grandma!" Sarah enjoyed emphasizing.

It was hard to believe what Grandma did on the trapeze up in the big tent. John Lincoln, (Mayor John Lincoln) called Sarah last Friday. He was laughing. The Cole Brothers Circus put their big tent up in the parking lot behind the Laurel Shopping Center, where parents had been bringing their children to have the circus experience every summer in Laurel for years. The ringmaster invited people from the audience to swing out over the net every performance. Sarah and her sibling remember watching classmates riding the elephants and swinging on the trapeze. Maybe some of them dared, but not Sarah. When the professionals and local daredevils were flying overhead, she looked in wonder and held tight to her seat.

"I tell you Sarah, when I saw Lucille Cotton go up that ladder with the trapeze artist, I thought I had seen everything. And when she swung out over my head, her dress went up and those boxer shorts with the big red heart in the crotch—I swear they were neon!" John Lincoln was laughing so hard he had to catch his breath. Sarah hung up on him.

Sarah took a deep breath and began.

"I called Grandma. She thought it was pretty smart to wear Grandpa's shorts on the trapeze. They were the shorts she gave him last year for Valentine's Day. Still in the box when she found them." Sarah took a breath and continued. "Nothing was *showing*. That surely made everything all right." She did not know what upset her more—getting this report from the mayor or Grandma's explanation.

"Grandma's our responsibility and I think if we worked to fill her life with things to keep her content, she wouldn't want to fly in the circus. All we need is for her to break her hip swinging on a trapeze." Sarah paused for emphasis.

Margaret was the only one laughing. The brothers said nothing. A closer look would have found Matt and Pete sharing a smile and the other brothers quickly pushing cookies in their mouths.

"Really, Maggie," she chastised, giving her sister a harsh glance. "A broken hip is serious at her age." Sarah brought the meeting back to her agenda.

Little old Grandma. Cute as a puppy and just as cuddly—the one thing they agreed on. They loved her dearly. She had been their champion and the center post in the family, especially for these baby boomers. Her role was grounded in the fact that she accepted their individuality, treated them with total honesty, and gave them room to keep growing, even in adulthood. Grandma had always led a conventional life but suddenly had become extravagant in her dress and adornment. Even at the grocery store, something sparkled on Grandma—a beaded blouse, a rhinestone hair clip, and always flashy earrings. She had a shelf at the top of the stairs lined with purses so she could change in an instant to match her shoes of many colors. Grandma had a standing hair appointment but refused the slight blue tint on white hair that was the fashion. Soft white

curls and Mamie Eisenhower bangs that *used to be* Grandma—
not anymore. At times, she had a streak of magenta or aqua
added to her tresses.

Mark swallowed his cookie before Sarah could get to her
agenda and offered. "Are we here to talk about Grandma living
alone since Grandpa died?"

"Let's just say that is one issue." Sarah answered in her offi-
cial voice.

Grandma lived alone on A Street, right off Main. Her home
was central to these grandchildren and always open to them.
The family had three generations living in Laurel, Maryland. She
was the matriarch; there were grandchildren and great-grandchildren. Several things prompted this meeting. Grandma never
seemed to be a problem to the family, but so much had changed
since Grandpa's death. Dad and Mom were supposed to take
care of Grandma and Grandpa. That was the plan, and it was far
into the future. But an airplane crash took Patrick and Joanne
Cotton. Earlier this year, Irving Cotton died. That left the younger generation without Grandpa or the middle generation—just
Grandma. The sweet old lady had gone in and out of their lives
at their convenience. Dad and Mom had been their safety net,
but now Grandma was out there swinging on the trapeze with
no one to catch her but this unruly gang of adult grandchildren.

If Patrick and Joanne had been here, they would have
known what to do, but Sarah, John, Mark, Pete, Matt, Jim, and
Margaret (plus Regina in Africa) hardly knew what to do with
their own lives.

Sarah put herself in charge. She was going to look just like
Grandma in a few decades. Right now, her thin, curly brown
hair has a few streaks of grey and a tightness around her mouth

that would never relax into the generous smile of the older woman. She was the classic dresser, typically beige slacks, navy blue blazer. The most colorful shoes in her wardrobe were a deep red pair of shoes to match the *wild* maroon knit dress. She had not worn it, nor the shoes, since they went into her closet. Bearing children rounded out her figure, and the softer Sarah was lovelier than the angular girl of school days. She decided that her looks were, at least, not repulsive. Sarah did not like to think about things for a long time. Nothing was as boring to Sarah as an unresolved problem. That is why she hated every cigarette she lit.

Calling this meeting was *typical* Sarah. She thought things over and then when she was sure she knew exactly what must be done, she would call her brothers and sisters in. She was always sure they would see wisdom in her solutions. They never did. How could they see the solution when they could not see the problem?

Grandma always said, "Sarah is the one who will jump out the window before the opening is cut in the wall." Everyone understood what Grandma meant except Sarah.

"I hate these meetings." Margaret went into the conclave. "The last one was over the headstone for Mom's grave. You had to have 'Never Forgotten' on it. Had to have it! You got your way, and every time I go to Ivy Hill and see it ... Joanne Cotton, Never Forgotten. Sounds like the damned *Song of the South*."

"Ok. Ok ..." Sarah tried to interrupt Margaret's tirade to no avail. "I'm going to get it changed; I told you ..."

"Come on Maggie; this meeting is important. We have a problem with Grandma." Matt wanted to move things along. As was their custom, the brothers ignored Sarah and Margaret's little disagreements, which were often about Margaret's colorful language. Mark's job was to make peace, but his mouth was full of chocolate chips and peanut butter cookies.

Sarah continued, "I am worried about that house being open to everyone, too. The key is under the mat. It doesn't take a brain surgeon to find it, and one of these days someone is going to break in or worse. The homeless on US 1 are wandering through there all the time. Winos, too. They could walk in looking for wine or money. I just can't stand the thought of Grandma being robbed or beaten. I dread the night we get the call that the police have been called to 206 A Street, and the money is gone from the dish cupboard and grandma has two black eyes or worse." Sarah was sure she had made her points. They were ready for her solution.

"There are seven of us, not counting Regina. If we divide the year up, each can have so many days to look out for her. I don't know any other way. She is like a child again—just like the children going up that ladder to the trapeze. Away she went. Too high for our 82-year-old grandmother." She added the last fact to emphasize her point and make sure no one forgot Grandma's age.

Then, a chorus filled the room.

"I can't do Christmas."

"Summer vacation."

"NASCAR race days."

"Baseball season."

"Super bowl."

"New Year's."

"Our cruise"

"Hold it." Sarah was at a loss. "Who has a calculator? What is 365 divided by 8?"

"45.6 days." Matt, the physicist, spoke up. "But that won't work; Regina is in Mozambique. She comes home for a week at Christmas and Easter. How can she take 45.6 days this year?"

"Maybe we should divide her another way." Pete, the lawyer, was about to get into the fray.

Jim asked, "Like how, stupid?" There is no respect for higher education among the siblings. "If we are going to do body parts, I don't want her mouth." Jim had his say.

One thing this group did well together was laughter. It was infectious among them, and they were not missing the humor in Grandma's circus act or Jim's words.

"This is getting a bit ridiculous. Let's go back to the beginning. Just what does Grandma need?" Pete, the lawyer, offered some common sense. "Does she need to be watched or would just a good *talking to* do it? Isn't she ever going to sit in a rocking chair or bake cookies? The house can be secured, and I think we should all spend more time with her."

Mark finally chimed in. "Let's take her to the senior center and see if she will get interested in the activities there."

"I took her to the Senior Center last week. I hope she finds something there she likes." Sarah was not ready to give up her plan. Since she was the one who worried about Grandma, she was sticking to her guns to get someone else to worry on a regularly scheduled basis. The truth is—the others did not worry about Grandma because Sarah did. "How about each of us taking a week on a seven-week rotation? John will do his part even if he isn't here today. Can't count on Regina. She could be in Timbuktu tomorrow. Check the schedule and see if your week falls on one of your favored activities. Get someone to switch with you if it does."

Matt saw that the only way to prove that this wasn't going to work was to try it. "I have a calendar. Let's start signing up. Who will take next week?"

"That's not good for me," was the unison reply.

"I will take care of Grandma next week, but each of you had better start thinking about this and be willing to take your turn. If this doesn't work, we will have to hire someone, and you will be coughing up the money to pay on a rotation every eight weeks. The least Regina can do is pay up." This was Sarah, of course.

That quieted the group, and Mark, the retired cryptologist and recently ordained deacon at St Mary's Catholic Church, took to the pulpit—actually, the fern stand—and began to pray. Since the brothers and sisters were not completely self-centered, they gave a minute of attention to their brother and God.

" ... and let us be ever mindful that You are watching over us and Grandma. Amen."

"Hey, I think we found the answer. Let God watch her." Margaret remarked as she slipped smoothly off the stool, pulled up her tight knee-high boots, and pulled down her tighter miniskirt. She checked her watch; she didn't want to be late getting her roots done and maybe climbing on another stool in a place with more atmosphere.

Margaret stepped to the door, opened it, and turned to address the dark, empty porch in a loud voice. "Oh, Here's Dad! Hi. Come in and tell us what you think of this conversation about Grandma. Are you proud of your children? Hugs and kisses, Dad. Ta ta." She walked through the non-existent spirit on the porch.

The meeting was over.

🀆 🀆 🀆

The beauty shop was buzzing when Margaret went in, and Amanda almost fell over herself getting to her. "Your Grandmother is in the tanning booth and she is getting an all-over tan. And I mean all over."

"Good God!' was her remark as if to chastise Him already for failing to do His job. Margaret went to the booth, but she wasn't prepared for what she saw. Grandma was glowing in the ultraviolet light, looking like a magazine centerfold published by AARP with a pair of oversized sunglasses she must have gotten from Elton John.

"I'll be finished soon. Sweetie," Lucille said, not recognizing her granddaughter.

"Grandma!" Margaret uttered in the lowest range her voice would go. Margaret would have gone straight to the phone to call Sarah, but she had to get her roots done.

Chapter 2

Lucille Cotton

The face looking back had aged. It was haggard, everything was sagging down, and what is that color—mousy grey?

"Grey. Everything is grey—my hair, my eyes, and my skin. I'm as antique as this old mirror!" Then Lucille Cotton did the first crazy thing. She took the mirror down and placed it in the coat closet facing the wall as if that would, somehow, change her image.

"I'm not the fairest in the land, that is for sure," she told Snow White, the cat. "I can eat apples without fear."

Lucille Cotton was not pleased with her appearance, but she was far from ugly. The family genes had been good to her. The beauty she had as a teenager was still remembered in her hometown. She was petite and aging, yes, but the sparkle in her eyes and the smile that dressed her pretty face had not aged, as had her hair color and skin. "Eighty-two," she repeated on the tread of each stirs she climbed. "Eight-two, not exactly a *mid-life* crisis."

On the second floor she had a nagging problem to address. Lucille had not removed Irving's clothes from the closet, and he died months ago. They needed to be packed up today for the Salvation Army pick-up. His shoes lined the wall like black and brown puppies. The old familiar aroma of his clothes assaulted her nose. Lucille stepped back against the door. She needed a moment. She turned her back on the emotion Irving's clothes brought and faced her own clothes hanging on the opposite wall. Her hand swept over the many items hanging there. "Ugh," she commented and did the second crazy thing today. She lifted them—dresses, skirts, blouses, ugly sweaters, hangers—and threw them to the floor beside the bed.

Lucille Cotton sat down on the bed and looked at the array of cotton, linen, polyester, and wool piled beside her. At the top of the pile was an emerald green pantsuit that she had worn on the anniversary cruise.

"I was something in that," she told Snow White, the cat, watching from her window perch. "I have gold slippers in here somewhere."

"Ah," she announced triumphantly as she hung the pant suit back on the empty rod on her side of the closet and placed the gold shoes carefully back on the shelf.

Down in the kitchen, the ever-ready electric teapot had hot water. It felt strange today, watching the tea bag go up and down in the mug—an out-of-body experience. Lucille felt like the tea bag trying to get the last bit of strength from the leaves. She did not want the tea; she did not want the mug. She definitely did not want to think about the closet upstairs and the clothes on the floor or sit in this kitchen alone and bob a lifeless teabag in hot water.

Lucille was still angry with Irving for dying and leaving her in this house. This house...

"Snow White," she invited her cat onto the chair, "you know how I feel about this house."

"I like this house," Snow White answered. "It's pretty tiresome listening to you complain about it."

"It's even worse now that Irving is gone. He loved this house." Lucille admitted.

"I'm not sure you hate the house or being in it alone. You loved that man, but you know I never did. Every time I came into the kitchen, he said he wanted a dog." Snow White pounced to the floor.

"He was only teasing about the dog."

"Pfissss. Irving Cotton always got his way. A dog could be at the bowl any day." Snow White continued as she went for the sunny spot in the dining room.

🐾 🐾 🐾

I rving told Lucille he was dying; she asked him not to go, but he went anyway. Irving was a good man, and she loved him, but dying was one more thing he did his way.

Lucille remembered the day they met when she fell in love with him. Her passion amazed him. He knew she only had her instincts to guide her. Innocent, she was. They married, and she thought she had everything she had ever wanted: a husband, a son, a daughter-in-law, and eight grandchildren to keep her busy. Fifty years later, Lucille realized she had not. She remembered exactly that moment, too.

Wearing the green pantsuit and gold slippers at the captain's table when the master of ceremonies introduced Lucille and Irving as celebrants of their 50th Anniversary. A special cake was brought to the table. The captain complimented her youthful, lovely appearance and accused Irving of robbing the cradle. To which Irving said, "You should have seen the one that got away." His old joke was appreciated by most of the people in the room.

Lucille knew she did not have everything she ever wanted.

When they got back to their stateroom, she told him.

"I never should have married you."

"Why did you wait so long to tell me?" Irving answered rhetorically .

Irving had completely forgotten the remark he made at dinner and was ignorant of her attitude. Lucille knew, although he did not mean to hurt her, he had failed to give her anything special for the anniversary except this meaningless cruise and futile attempt at humor. He made light of her regrets and continued. "I could have gone into the astronaut program." He turned his attention to the fancy gift basket on the table presented by the Princess Cruise Line. "Let's open this bottle of Champaign, and I will let you rub my aching back."

In all their years, she never missed the chance to be near him and touch him because, generally, he did not like to be touched. Ironically, in the last few years, as cancer chipped away his health, he wanted her near, and he wanted her to hold his hand and move close in bed. During the last year, they fell asleep cuddled together. She loved every minute of his wanting her—way beyond that old sexual need that she clearly remembered. That was how their life was. Love but no romance and certainly no adventure. Small hurts but no anger. Now she wondered who she was and what it was that she really wanted all those years that Irving kept from her.

When she packed to go home from the cruise, she resolved never to wear the green outfit and gold slippers again. She placed them in the suitcase next to Irving's many medications and his ever-present final directive, reminding her of a new and old reality packed together.

♣ ♣ ♣

Lucille dipped the tea bag one more time and let it drip, ripple after ripple, in her cup. The sharp rapping on the door brought her out of her revelry and back to today.

"Good morning," said the Salvation Army truck driver. "You have a pickup for us? I don't see anything on your porch."

"Good morning, young man. Yes, I do have things for you. Can you help me bring them from upstairs?"

"We aren't supposed to do that, Ma'am."

"Oh, I see. Well, could you stand right here at the foot of the stairs? I'll throw them down."

The stairs were just two steps away. The driver paused and thought about his own grandmother. Erroneously, he concluded this sweet old lady was too frail to carry bags down those steps.

"OK. I guess I can do that," he responded.

The scene that followed was, to say the least, overwhelming to the accommodating young man. Lucille went upstairs and began throwing her clothes down, hangers and all—dresses, skirts, blouses, sweaters, and robes. Then Irving's suits, pants, jackets, shirts, and favorite flannels came down in a flurry. Ties, pajamas, socks, belts, suspenders, undershirts, and boxers fell like snow drifting in, filling the stairwell to the eighth step.

"Wait! Wait! "The driver yelled, but Grandma was too deep into the closet to hear as shoes began falling. The truck driver had to defend himself, using his elbows to deflect Irving's' heavy shoes, and then, her pointed toes and heels came like hail. By now, the whole stairwell was full of the entire contents of the walk-in closet that Lucille and Irving Cotton had shared.

"Lordy," Grandma exclaimed as she looked down at the Salvation Army driver, waist-deep in garments and overcome with laughter. The whole avalanche took less than five minutes and rivaled the snow sliding down the mountain at Lake Tahoe. She stepped down two steps to push things out of the way so she could descend. She stepped on a slipper that had only begun to go down the ski trail, lost her balance, and slowly slid down the slope to the waiting arms of Sonny Perkins, Salvation Army driver, first day on the job.

She looked into his eyes, which were now level with hers, and said, "I'm Lucille Cotton. Nice catch."

"I'm Sonny Perkins, catcher for the PG County Fireman's Softball Team. Glad to oblige. Here you are, Mrs. Cotton." He set her down away from the avalanche.

"I'll get some bags so we can pack up this ah . . . donation," Sonny took charge at last.

It took a while to stuff it all into twelve bags and stow them on the truck. While he was doing that, she made him some iced tea and tuna sandwiches to go. He promised to come back for dinner on Tuesday and left amazed at the morning he spent with the *frail* old woman.

"See you Tuesday at six and bring your girl." Lucille Cotton sat on the porch and watched the truck go down A Street, turn left on Main, heading for US 1 and away with all of Irving's personal items and all the dressings that made Lucille an old, grey, drab-looking widow.

I am old, the 82-year-old woman said to herself. *But I'm not dead yet.* She sat in the mid-morning sun and thought about what she had done and why she did it. It was the realization that she did not have to explain it to Irving that brought her to a straight-back posture. "Irving, "she addressed him, "I loved you. I did everything to be a good wife, and I miss you. I hope you can see me now. And if you can, you will finally see me do things that *I* want to do." Snow White looked up at her. "I'm not speaking to you. Don't say a word, you lazy cat. Go back to your nap."

It was remarkable that she could even think about changing her life and be happy after the last two difficult years. Only Irving's death could take her mind off grieving for the loss of their son and daughter-in-law in a tragic airplane crash coming home from a vacation in Tennessee fifteen months ago. That was a lot of tragedy. The missing generation put a hole in her family, and Lucille had to learn to relate directly to her adult grandchildren, their spouses, and an array of great-grandchildren. That was her challenge and even more difficult than finding her way without Irving.

Lucille had the choice of looking backward or looking forward, and she chose forward. *Grief is a strange bedfellow. It brings you down and makes you want to escape. And yet, it beckons you on at the same time.*

"I'm going to Hecht's and buy a red dress." Lucille went into the house, talking to herself and Snow White.

Snow White looked back at her and took a stance by sitting in the doorway.

"Now, don't get testy with me, Snow. I don't have time to talk to you now. Move so I don't trip." The cat slowly vacated the pathway and put her long furry tail into the air. "It's a good thing I got dressed before Sonny got here, or I wouldn't have anything to wear to go shopping." It was her habit to keep Snow White informed and hope for her approval.

"Nothing black. Nothing brown. Nothing grey and nothing navy blue," the cat advised as she continued to the sunny spot in the kitchen.

With a new spirit in her step, Lucille combed her hair and got her purse for the short trip to the Laurel Shopping Center. She was careful in her driving and parking and took time to be sure her key was in her purse when she locked the door. *While I'm being foolish, no use in being foolish,* she thought and laughed out loud. Lucille knew her age slowed her down, and she might forget where she parked, and carelessness would cause the key to be locked in the car. With the same determination that emptied her closet, she was ready to change her outward appearance and begin her new, free life.

She entered the only department store in Laurel and within the limits of her driving range. As she started for the *Ladies'* department, Lucille looked into the *Juniors* and stopped in her tracks. Today, she would not go past the lively, colorful clothes in the *Juniors* department. Her tiny figure could fit these clothes if she chose. Lucille had kept her weight to 126 pounds, but she was a bit thick through the middle, and as Irving often reminded—her buttock was on a lower level. She faced those realities but insisted that her frame was still 5' 3".

"I'll shop in the Juniors!" She proclaimed to no one.

"May I help you?' asked the clerk.

"No, I'm just looking."

"Shopping for your granddaughter?"

"No, for myself." The clerk made herself busy elsewhere.

Lucille loved the new spring colors and styles with glossy patent belts, some with chains, and layered blouses. It intrigued her that Juniors wore pants at every length. She could choose long, ankle, calf, and even knee length and she did, in colors of sherbet. Lucille could hardly resist anything in peacock blue.

The clerk at the jewelry counter had great fun pulling out necklaces to match the new purchases and even some gold chains in the newer, longer length. Lucille let her know right away if she presented anything that was too *old*. The purchases were rung up and paid for with the credit card that Irving never let her use. Moreover, for using it, she got an extra 15 % off.

"How nice, my dear," she said. "Please hold these here while I go to the lingerie department."

"Maybe you should go to *Old Navy*." the clerk said under her breath. Lucille heard and nodded in agreement. She bought a new robe that looked very tropical and pajamas that would have kept Irving awake.

Lucille was worn out; shopping was exhausting, and it built an appetite. She collected her packages and accepted the help of a clerk to get them to the car. When she got home, she wished she had Sonny Perkins to help her get everything in the house and up the stairs.

🦋 🦋 🦋

Meanwhile, Sarah was busy at the bookstore. She decided to get some books for Grandma. *Our National Parks, Scenic Wonders of America, America's Capitol City, Everyone Loves NYC,* and *Spain, the Magical Place.* She went from the bookstore to Goodwill and did some serious shopping. She bought a wooden rocker and a floor lamp that fit nicely in her van. One more stop at the dollar store for a comfy cushion. Feeling very good about her mission, Sarah headed to Grandma's house.

Lucille and Irving raised their son, Patrick, on A Street and stretched the small place to accommodate eight grandchildren for dinners and sleepovers. It is one of a row of identical houses on this street where the mill workers had lived in the early 1900s. Two stories with a dirt-floor cellar. Irving had added a small room on the back behind the kitchen for a bedroom a few years after he retired so they would not have to climb stairs. Lucille decided she would rather climb the stairs than sleep with the old fart and the new farts that he enjoyed blasting nightly.

The houses on this street had changed, and now they sported various sidings and expanded with enclosed porches. Lucille had lived in this house for over 50 years and hated it for all but the first three months of that time. Every time Lucille said to Irving, "Let's move," he would laugh. After a few years, she took to slapping a glancing blow on his head whenever they had this one-sided conversation. Soon, she got the newspaper and stood behind him when she said, "Let's move," he chuckled, and she put a glancing blow across his bald head. *Whop!* There was no way for Irving to escape this torment. She was not going to stop asking him to move. He did not consider stopping the newspaper because he enjoyed reading it. Besides, it didn't really hurt, and she didn't do it every day. It was a marital ritual that somehow cemented the relationship just as pinching her butt whenever he had the chance.

Sarah lifted the doormat, got the key, and went in with her purchases. It took several trips to get it all set up, with the rocker near the heat register, and the floor lamp in just the right spot behind and to the left for easy reading. She emptied the magazine rack of Grandpa's dusty periodicals and filled it with the books she had selected. Then she pulled the small round table from the hall, thinking that Grandma would want to set her tea there. As Sarah admired her tableau, she heard Grandma coming in the back door.

"Yoo-hoo! Grandma, I'm here. Did you see my car out front?"

"Yes, dear. What are you doing, Sarah?" she said as she shook her red curls.

"Grandma, what big red curls you have!" Sarah exclaimed, not knowing how much she sounded like Steven Sondheim.

"I told Amanda. Bernadette Peters curls. Just what I wanted. They are really good at the New Image Salon." She touched them lovingly and smiled at herself. Sarah almost forgot about the things she had brought to make a change in Grandma's life.

"What's this?" Grandma asked, noticing the additions to her room

"I found the rocker in Goodwill and thought how comfortable it looks." Sarah sat in the rocker, shifted on the cushion, and tilted her head back.

"Relax, dear, and I will get you some tea." Sarah's efforts were not in vain.

"I thought you would enjoy some armchair traveling, Grandma. I got you some books and set this up for you."

"Thank you, dear. Drink your tea. I have some things to put away upstairs. I'll only be a few minutes. We can visit." She would love to tell Sarah about Sonny Perkins and her shopping spree today.

"I can't stay. I'll leave the tea here for you. Love you," Sarah shouted as she moved to the door.

"Lock up when you leave, and don't forget to put the key back under the mat. Never know when someone may need to come in. Thanks . . . . and I love you, too."

Lucille enjoyed hanging her new clothes in the empty closet.

"Snow White, I spent $807.86," she reported to the cat as she reviewed the receipt. That was barely a ripple in Irving's life insurance policy, which was deposited yesterday. More money than they had ever had, plus his pension. It was more than she would be able to spend.

Snow White climbed onto the toilet seat to watch Lucille brush her teeth and wash her face.

"Well?" she asked.

"Well, what?" Lucille responded.

"Are you going to explain your hair to me?" Snow continued.

"I know, I know. It seems a little crazy."

"A little," Snow White agreed.

"I like it, and I may not keep this very long but right now—it works for me. Don't you like red curls?" Lucille ran her fingers through her hair and checked her reflection before heading to bed.

Snow White followed, took her place on the bed, and waited.

"If I don't do what I want to do now, I never will. You know I have never been happy conforming. And that's what I have done all my life. A bit of red in my hair, some colorful clothes and some new activities. What's wrong with that?" Lucille stroked the cat's head and relaxed.

"Absolutely nothing. You may surprise your grandchildren, but you don't surprise me. You need to take care of yourself, and it isn't your job to make everyone else comfortable. I've watched you comforting all these years. Losing Patrick and Joanne. Then Irving. You could not be the same person any longer." Snow began to purr.

"I'm glad you understand. I loved Irving so much." Lucille sighed. "Loved him so much and yet, I was not happy in the marriage. I became invisible, colorless and irrelevant."

"Doing everything everyone wanted you to do. And being everything everyone wanted you to be. It's a great way to lose yourself." Snow told Lucille what she needed to hear, before they both drifted off to sleep.

The next morning, Lucille stopped at the coat closet to retrieve the mirror she had banished yesterday. She hung it back on the nail still in the wall. Looking into it she saw a smiling face; most of the lines around the mouth and eyes were accenting her attitude and did not look so cavernous. Her color was pink, and cheeks were rosy with excitement for the changes and decisions she had made.

"I look 75. Actually 70, with red curls," she said, stroking her hair and admiring the person looking back at her in the mirror.

Lucille picked up the book, *Spain, The Magical Place* and went to make her tea in the fine china cup—no more mugs – without even glancing at the rocking chair.

She did not have the slightest twinge of doubt about her activities yesterday. For the first time she thought about her grandchildren. Sarah, John, Mark, Jim, Pete, Matt, Regina, and

Margaret. She was absolutely, positively, sure they would not understand. That gang of baby boomers, all born during the late 40's and 50's, and spoiled by their parents, would think she had *lost* her mind. They would never believe, as she did, that she had *found* something more important. If there is anything she loved completely, it is that bunch of mixed-up young adults. If there was anything she loved doing, it was stirring them up and making them grow and learn.

"They aren't too old to grow up and change. I did," she proclaimed to the first ray of sun and Snow White.

Chapter 3

Snow White

Irving brought a stray kitten home from work one day. It was covered in soot after being rescued from a chimney in a house his company was demolishing.

"I brought you a gift, Sweety," he announced as if it were roses and chocolates.

"A cat! Absolutely not. I don't want a cat underfoot. Take it to Animal Welfare." Lucille was adamant. "No black cats in this house," she insisted.

As usual, Irving did not listen to her. He took some shampoo to the hose and managed to bathe the cat—a miracle in itself.

"Look, Lucy, the cat isn't black. Meet Snow White." He put the kitten in Lucille's lap. And that was that.

It was almost a month later, after Snow White selected Lucille to love, and Lucille began to love Snow White, that the kitten turned her head up and said, "Thank you."

"What?" Lucille asked as a joke, sure she had imagined it.

"Thank you," Snow White repeated.

Lucille picked Snow White up, letting her paws and legs dangle and looking her in the eyes. "Cats don't talk," she announced.

"I do. Please. Put me down."

Lucille dropped Snow White. She landed on her feet as cats always do. Lucille tried to tell Irving that Snow White talked.

"What did she say?" Irving laughed.

"Thank you, and please." Lucille answered.

Before he left the room laughing, he mumbled. "Don't tell anyone your cat can talk. They will send you to the crazy farm. Unless you can convince Johnny Carson to put you and Snow White on his show."

Chapter 4

Pete and Matt

Matt had the academic mind. This was contested by Pete, who was, after all, a lawyer. It makes him a little ill to see his brother write the *PhD* with his signature as if it was something everyone needed to know.

Matt looks like a mathematician—a complicated figure of xx's and ++'s—multiplicitous, fragile, stick figure scratched on a chalkboard—easily erased and rebuilt. Matthew Cotton, PhD.

It is well established that Pete has a good mind, too. But more than that, he can think on his feet, make a mahogany desk seem small, and earn lots of money. Pete graduated Laurel High School, tied with Matt for valedictorian. He did an undergrad degree in three years, got his law degree, and passed the bar on his own accelerated schedule. Peter Jacob Cotton, JD.

Otherwise known as *The Twins*.

Pete and Matt were fraternal twins, bearing only slight resemblances. Matt is small with delicate features like Lucille. Pete has Irving's 6-foot stature and childish grin. Both have

Grandma's prematurely white hair—each, in his own way, handsome. Last year, they showed up at the family 4th of July picnic sporting beards. Simultaneously to each other they said, "What's with the beard?" It was another of those classic Matt/ Pete moments when denying their twinship was impossible and making the rest of the family shake their heads. Actually, they looked more alike with beards.

Two days after Sarah's family meeting, Pete called Matt. "Can you do lunch at the club on Tuesday and bring Grandma?" Pete enjoyed hosting at his club somewhat like Matt writing PhD after his name. His country club had congressmen and political bigwigs. He played golf with the Washington correspondent for NBC and called several well-known authors by their first name.

"I already invited her. She will be ready at noon. Let's see firsthand what Sarah is going on about. We don't want her to hurt herself or embarrass us. Can you pick her up?"

"Sure. What are we going to say to her?"

"Well, for one thing, we will talk about that trapeze thing, and now Sarah says she is training for the Senior Olympics. Equestrian, no less. Do you know what horses do in the Olympics?"

"Not a clue."

"Sarah called the Gorman Road Stables. Grandma is enrolled in a program sponsored by the Senior Olympics Committee. I want to know what that is all about. Maybe we can get her to tone down her dress a bit and act more appropriately for her age."

"Anyone else in on this lunch?"

"Absolutely not. Just us. No need to cloud the issues with the others."

The twins were middle children. What could be expected—competitive, brainy, intelligent, overachievers and family-confused. How did they get into this family to begin with? It was the one thing they agreed on—by mistake. As children they spent a lot of time speculating how they got the wrong parents and who their real parents were. A study of their siblings just reinforced the doubt. Being intelligent they could analyze their traits and see the missing links. For instance, neither one liked milk. This was important because each of the brothers could wipe out a gallon of milk at one meal. Mom was the only person in the world who confused them. Matt was called *Pete.* Pete was called *Matt.* Any natural mother would know her sons apart. They never seemed to notice that John, Mark, and Jim suffered the same name fumbling from their mother. The most important clue was their brains. No one in the family had the brainpower of these two. They could outthink, outmaneuver, and outwit everyone. They stopped discussing their parentage at about age eleven but secretly each still believed some strange twist of fate had put them in this family. In addition, they didn't believe they were really twins. Pete and Matt would never know who their real family was. Now after passing through their mid-life crisis and analysis, they accepted their fate and loved the family.

Although Pete and Matt spent most of their lives proving they were different, they often did things simultaneously which amazed them and entertained the family. Often, they started to move at once, tangling feet and falling over each other. This was not a rare occurrence when they were children. As adults they try not to stand in proximity. Unless forced to by events, they never sat next to one another. But fate would not allow them to totally escape this phenomenon, and they occasionally landed on the floor together, white hair, beards, and all.

Lucille was delighted to go to the Congressional Country Club for lunch with Matt and Pete, the most clueless of her grandchildren. The Country Club meant dressing up, and she loved the chance to go beyond her everyday wardrobe.

"Lunch at your club? I'd love to. Tell Matt I'll be ready when he comes for me on Tuesday," Grandma responded enthusiastically. *It is always fun watching these two acting so smart while they get everything wrong,* she thought as she hung up the phone from Pete's call.

She loved the boys dearly, and if she played favorites, the twins would be close to the top.

Dressing for her date took all morning. First, a stop at New Image to get her color touched up and her curls tightened. Today, she would get make-up done and her nails, too. Amanda knew a good thing when she saw it and talked Grandma into false eyelashes—$29.99. The total for today was $64.99. Today, like every appointment in the past, Amanda asked, "Send the bill to Irving?" Lucille nodded. She knew she would write the check herself but enjoyed the little fantasy that Irving would be at the desk fussing about the bill again.

Lucille selected the green pantsuit from the cruise. Maybe it would get a new significance at this lunch date with Pete and Matt. The wide collar and bell-bottom pants with black topstitching in big, wide stitches would look great today. The bright green color was perfect with her hair, that turned out slightly more orangy-blond. She was less Bernadette Peters and more Carol Burnett—smaller version. Lucille decided to ignore the gold shoes in favor of the conservative black shoes and purse, plus black onyx jewelry.

Matt's eyes popped when he saw her, and Grandma knew she had made all the right choices.

"Matt, dear. I am looking forward to lunch with you and Pete. Is it all right if I bring a friend? He will be here any minute. Oh, there he is now. Fredrico, my equestrian coach."

Matt did not know what to say except, "Let's go." In his mind, he was enjoying the fact that Pete would probably go ballistic over this added lunch guest. He could not help but notice how handsome Fredrico was. Grandma made the introductions and proceeded to talk all the way to the club.

Pete *wanted* to go ballistic when he saw Grandma and her guest, but this was *his* club, and making a scene would never happen. Instead, he led them to his favored table overlooking the water feature on the seventh hole, requested an extra place setting, and seated his grandmother in a gentlemanly fashion.

"Pete, this is Fredrico, my riding instructor." Nods between the men completed the introduction.

"So, you are a horseman ... what do equestrians do in the Olympics?" Pete began his examination as they were taking their places.

"Fredrico doesn't speak English." Grandma offered with a big smile for her guest.

"Great. He doesn't speak English?"

"That's right, dear. He just needs a good lunch." Pete's face was scarlet. His blood pressure went through the roof. The white hair and beard surrounding his red face resembled a strawberry shortcake. Without looking up, Pete snapped his napkin and threw it across his lap. "Let's order."

Grandma, Matt, and Pete each had a specialty salad. Fredrico pointed to his selection on the menu. By some good luck, he selected the crabcake platter and smiled in delight when two plump golden Maryland delicacies were placed in front of him.

Pete noticed women in the room took notice of Fredrico's dark good looks. Some golf wives, who usually barely acknowledged him, came by the table to speak and smile at Fredrico. The waitress waited at his elbow.

Grandma treated Fredrico like a grandchild, so they were not concerned about her interest in him. However, the twins were wondering.... *what was Fredrico's interest in Grandma?* They had a way of communicating without words, and the puzzled looks on their faces were identical.

They concluded it was good that Fredrico did not speak English. Their conversation with Grandma could begin without concern about it being understood by a stranger.

"Grandma, we wanted to talk to you about some family things."

"Good. I wanted to talk to you about the same subject. Who goes first?" Grandma responded with a smile.

"You, Grandma." Pete, the lawyer, master of words in his profession, knew it would be best to hear her first because rebuttal was his genre.

"Pete, you and Matt have made, you-know-what's of yourselves as long as I can remember. I love you very much, but you were a problem from the minute you were born and decided you couldn't wait for your mother to get to the hospital. Right there in the living room, your heads popped out. I thought then, these two will go against the grain."

"Wait. . . Wait. . . Grandma, are you saying we were born at home? We have a photo of Mom bringing us home from PG County Hospital. One on each arm." Matt interrupted. This was a new story, one they had never heard before.

"Yes, You were taken there to be checked out, but you were born at home. Right away—stirring things up in this family." Grandma hardly noticed the looks Pete and Matt exchanged. They seemed to be having trouble swallowing their food.

Grandma continued. " I have waited and waited for you to be team players. As you have scrambled to outdo one another, you have separated yourself from your brothers and sisters. When the others want to work together, you two want to go your own way. And when it is just the two of you, you work against each other. Even as children, when there were games—card games or games in the yard—we could never decide if you should be on the same team or opposing teams; it didn't matter. You never helped anyone win unless it was at the expense of your brother." She paused to look out at the beautiful golf course. "Pete, look at that golf course. It is more important to you than anything. I think that's because golf is a game for the individual. Don't have to be a team player out there. But what do I know? What is Sylvia doing today? Bet you don't even know."

Amazingly Grandma was managing to eat while this tirade was going on. By holding her left forefinger in the air while she took a bite, the two men seemed suspended as she ate her lunch and continued talking. On the other hand, they were not eating much of their salad. Fredrico was doing well with his lunch with the very attentive young waitress standing by to keep him happy in case he would favor her with a smile. Pete didn't have time to be disgusted about that, he had to pay attention to Grandma.

"I guess Sylvia is shopping...." He seemed to be speaking from some far-off land. He forgot about his rebuttal.

"And Matt . . . what is all that math and science doing for

you? After being married twenty-five years. One ex-wife and no children. That sure doesn't add up in my book. What did you do with her when you had her? 'PhD'! Pshaw! You should be minding your 'Ps' and 'Qs'." Grandma hardly drew a breath, raised her finger, and took another bite. "In case you don't know, P's and Q's means procreation quota."

Pete and Matt choked on that statement. Grandma had been waiting a long time to deliver this clever line that she had read in *Readers' Digest.*

"Eat your lunch, boys." She assumed her Grandmotherly role and returned to her salad.

Fredrico did not miss a bite but kept looking from one to the other of his fellow diners, watching the looks on their faces. He was the only one who saw one of Grandma's eyelashes fall onto the salad plate and go into her mouth. He laughed, but since he was invisible at the table—he laughed alone.

"This is a wonderful lunch. My salad is delicious and has wonderful crunchies in it." Grandma commented. One of the crunchies just cost Irvin Cotton, deceased, $14.98. "I hope you will invite me again, but I must say, think about the way you dress next time." Pete and Matt put their forks down at the exact same moment. They had had enough salad.

"Matt, don't look so frumpy. And Pete, you're dressed like an undertaker. I am almost embarrassed to be out with you. You could be buried in those clothes. I don't want it said of me that I dressed the same dead as alive."

"Never happen," Matt whispered to himself.

"Look at me. My clothes will have to be changed before they put me in the wooden box. Do you see the lesson here?"

The waiter interrupted her spiel, "Dessert menu and coffee?'

The two brothers issued a prayer. "Thank God."

Fredrico was the first to say "Buena," as he reached for the menu. "Chocolate."

"I see your friend knows English for menu."

Four coffees were ordered, along with one pecan pie and one Devilish Double Chocolate Mousse Brownie with vanilla ice cream and caramel syrup. As Grandma began eating the pie and Fredrico admired his chocolate mound, Pete *finally* went with his closing remarks.

"Grandma, Matt and I will take your suggestions about our clothes on advisement. We want to talk about you. We are worried that some of the things you are doing could be dangerous. Swinging on a trapeze? Would you ever do that again?"

"Nope. Once was enough." She picked up the fork.

"Now you want to ride a horse in the Senior Olympics. You don't know how to ride a horse. This isn't the time for you to begin horseback riding."

"Don't talk to me about time. I have a good handle on time. Do you?" Grandma charged as she turned the pie plate around and around, savoring the beauty of her chosen desert.

Pete ignored her interruption and went on with his prepared remarks.

"I'm not talking about time; I'm talking about riding a horse. There are other sports more fitting for . . ."

"An old lady?" She asked as she cleared a piece of pie from the fork.

"Things not as dangerous as horseback riding," Matt added.

"Like what?" Another bite; without looking up.

"Well ... swimming." Pete was thinking on his feet.

"Can't swim." This was the best pecan pie she had ever

eaten. Pete and Matt stumbling around made it taste even better. What a wonderful lunch.

"We could get a coach to teach you, and he will speak English." It had to be Pete to suggest something that would cost money. Matt's alimony kept him broke.

"I've got a coach." She smiled at Fredrico who smiled back—a rich chocolate smile.

"We mean a swimming coach." Matt was letting frustration filter into his voice, but she ignored it. That was part of the fun.

"Swimming would mess my hair. Chlorine isn't good for Bernadette Peters curls. Besides Fredrico is a wonderful coach. I picked horses. Not speaking English makes him perfect. He nods agreement to everything. I like being around positive people. May have to stay away from you kids. You're all too negative." The last bite of pie had a generous portion of pecans, filling, and the flakey crust. Grandma was satiated.

This lunch had not gone well. Neither Matt nor Pete knew what had happened. Their two guests had had a wonderful meal and time. They were full and happy as they rose from the comfortable seats and thanked the attentive waitress.

"Gracias, Gracias," Grandma said, speaking for herself and Fredrico.

The twins shared acid reflux, sour stomachs, and headaches. Pete canceled his golf game. He would love a scotch on the rocks, but he knew better than to put alcohol in his stomach when it was burning. It is the same burning he gets when he loses a case. *I'll go see what Syl is doing today,* he decided.

Matt dropped Grandma and Fredrico off at A Street. He decided not to call Pete and tell him Grandma's parting remark. "Fredrico also teaches bullfighting in Madrid."

Snow White was full of questions about the lunch with Pete and Matt. But Lucille did not invite a conversation with her cat.

"Tell me. Tell me," Snow insisted.

"Not now, Snow White. I'm tired."

Chapter 5

Margaret

It was the weekly appointment at New Image that brought Margaret to Amanda's chair. Today was a long appointment so she could get a new hair color.

"Hi Amanda. Do your magic and make my day wonderful."

Amanda could tell by the way Margaret plopped herself into the chair that they would have to cover some ground before the day's task could begin.

Margaret was in tight jeans, and plopping was the only way to get into the chair—bending was impossible. She did look good in them, and the tight denim held in the tiny bulge that pregnancy and age had left about four inches below her waist. The knit blouse had a plunging neckline, and Margaret had filled it with beads and chains of all lengths, up to chokers. They hid a lot of neck wrinkles. She was a hen—not a chick. Youngest in her family but not out in the world. Amanda was one of the few people who got to see pictures of Margaret's grown children.

"You're lookin' good."

"Thanks." Margaret always warmed up to a compliment. Today's malcontent was not aimed at Amanda.

"OK. What is happening?" Amanda asked as she picked up Margaret's shoulder-length locks and let them fall through her fingers.

"It's a hell of a note when you can't get the hair color you want because your Grandmother got it first." Amanda knew better than to laugh and only then remembered Margaret talking of going red this month. She had to smile when she recalled the old lady leaving with Bernadette Peters' curls yesterday.

"I guess I will stay blond until things settle down. I wanted to be a red head again. Even went out and bought some clothes in the fall colors to set it off. Bring out the color board, and let's see what you've got."

Hours later Margaret left the shop with a darker blond color but with lots of lighter high lights—some gold, some amber. It was very becoming and younger looking. Both women were pleased with the reflection in the mirror.

Amanda sighed in relief and took a long draw on her cigarette and diet Coke.

Instead of going home to her empty home, Margaret decided to head to Sam's for a cold one and the best hamburger in town. She had ways to fight loneliness, and going to Sam's was one of them. This bar had some of the best food in town. It was a little-known secret in Laurel except among the regulars and the owners and trainers who came whenever the horses ran at the Laurel Racetrack.

When Margaret entered that doorway, she cut quite a figure, and most men noticed her immediately. It was easy to place her age up close, but from a distance, she could look as young as 20, depending on how many beers the men had consumed. She was not about fooling them so much as she was about turning their heads, and she could do that. Most of the people in Sam's knew Margaret. She waited for her eyes to become accustomed to the dim light before deciding where she would sit. After nodding to the patrons she knew, Margaret went to the empty end of the bar, where she would have a chance to talk to Nora, the owner. At the opposite end of the bar sat one patron she did not know, but he was far enough away not to bother her. Nora brought Margaret her usual beer and cheeseburger.

Margaret and Nora have been friends since first grade. It felt comfortable with an old girlfriend, familiarity, and a cold beer. Margaret came often through the years. Sam's was an easy place to unwind after work as the business manager at the Transit Truck Stop on US 1 for 14 years. Margaret got the job out of High School and was a hard worker. She picked up her colorful language during those years. She could cuss like a sailor, except she did not use the four-letter word. It would be too risky. That taboo word that might become a habit and fall out at a bad time. A good manager at the truck center had to talk to the drivers and the trucking companies with whatever style of language they needed. Margaret took adult education courses at night to learn Spanish, which she picked up easily, and found it as valuable as her salty language.

The best thing Margaret picked up at the truck stop was Larry. She had been divorced for seven years when he walked into the truck stop and began his campaign to win her.

"How about lunch?"

"Thanks, but I've had lunch."

"How about dinner."

"No thanks, I have plans."

"How about tomorrow?" She shook her head.

"Thursday? Friday?"

"Mr. Hamilton, I have this rule. I don't make dates at work."

Margaret was not interested in the owner of one of the biggest trucking lines that had an account with Transit. He was a bothersome man. She knew his type. They showed up often when you work on US Highway 1.

Larry could see why a looker like her had to draw the line, so he waited until she was in her car at 5:40 to approach her again. "You off work?"

She had to laugh at his persistence. "I'm off work and on my way to Sam's"

"Sam your friend's or Sam's—the restaurant?" She had to laugh again; he was quick. He followed her to Sam's—the restaurant—and opened the door for her. Nora greeted them with a raised brow. She had never seen these two customers together before.

"Hi Maggie....Larry!" Nora greeted them.

Larry was persistent and charming. He gave her the bums rush, wined, dined her for two weeks, and then stayed away. It was an old trick that usually worked. He wanted her to miss the fine things he had done for her and hopefully miss him, too.

Margaret did. The next time he called, she was between excited to get the call and angry at being ignored.

"I have missed you, Margaret. I have been trying not to see you, but it isn't working. Can I pick you up after work today?"

"How about my place? 6:30?" She wanted to take her car home and dress for him. They settled into warm evenings and great conversations. From that day and time, they were a couple. Larry was serious and in it for keeps. Margaret had never considered a permanent relationship. She enjoyed her independence since her divorce. Larry had to convince her that marriage would work. He could take very good care of her.

"Margaret, will you marry me." He proposed the first time after three months together. Almost weekly he continued to propose. "We can have it all. We can do it all. We can travel. We can have a home wherever you want. We can be....everything together. Aren't you tired of *being out there,* as they say?" He went on with his argument, "I love you and want to grow old with you. " Margaret had thought about growing old and didn't like the prospect—not with Larry or anybody. She was sure with all his resources they would not have to grow old. The best California plastic surgeons, the spas of Italy, and the gym on the corner of Montgomery and US 1 would keep them young. He wanted to give her the moon, but instead, he gave her early retirement from the Truck Stop, a very generous allowance, and all the spa time and plastic surgery she wanted.

"I want to make you happy." As he said the words, she realized, more than his promises, Margaret did not want to be alone any longer. Larry changed her world. His promises were honest, and their intimacy natural and fulfilling. Margaret was surprised to be satisfied. After many weeks and many months, she expected to wake up one morning and be discontented or anxious to move on. She believed sooner or later, she would want her independence again. It never happened. And so, after one more proposal, she accepted and put that big diamond on her third finger, left hand. Life was grand, good, and plush. Margaret fell in love with Larry and by their first anniversary, she was head over heels for her husband. It was Broadway plays and New Orleans' beignets. It was San Francisco's Chinatown, Palm Beach, and Caribbean dunes. They traveled to Europe and did the Mexican resorts. He was right; they could have it all and a good marriage too.

One evening, coming home from Meyerhof Concert Hall, they took a shortcut down Route 216, and she pointed to a beautiful brick home on a manicured lawn. "That has always been my dream house."

Larry bought her the house and gave it to her as a surprise for their third anniversary.

"I didn't know it was for sale."

"It wasn't but as they say in the *Godfather*, 'I made an offer they couldn't refuse.'"

She could have asked for a villa or a mansion in some exclusive neighborhood, but instead, she wanted a lovely home right across the river from her hometown. Close to family but not too close. Margaret was delighted to decorate; Larry landscaped. Margaret found it easy to be happy in Laurel with Larry. They planned and traveled but not at a fever pitch. They began to acknowledge each other in small pleasures.

Before their fourth anniversary, Larry had a massive heart attack and was gone. Margaret had her dream home and all his money, but she would give it all back to have Larry again. Along with all he left her, Larry left Margaret lonely.

Now after five years on her own, Margaret had had plenty of experience in bars. She could pick 'em up, and she could put 'em down as she referred to the men she met. The game had lost its charm, and it was rare that a man of interest caught her attention. As much as she hated to admit it, most men she met these days were boys.

Tonight's cheeseburger was good. It was better than good; it was great. One of the few places left where they pat their own ground beef and caramelize the onions. Another beer would go well. Margaret was mellowing out and beginning to think about going home and taking an aroma bath when she was startled from her revelry.

"Mind if I sit here?" It was posed with a Latin accent by a stranger who had moved from the other end of the bar.

"It's a free country."

"May I buy you a beer?"

"No, I've had enough."

"Are you from around here? I need some directions." She was much too wise for this line; he could have asked Nora. He didn't have to come over here to ask directions. Margaret decided to ignore him, finish her sandwich and beer, and move on. He sure was good looking—she had to admit.

He sat there with his beer and did not say another word. He got very interested in his drink and the TV above the bar.

That did it. The nerve of him ignoring her after making that pass. She had to think about this, eat her cheeseburger more slowly, and sip the beer. He will make another pass; they always do. But he didn't. Margaret thought about it long and hard; had she been rude, or had he? She laughed out loud, and he looked at her.

"Have I been rude? I'm sorry. Where are you going? I know Laurel inside and out." She broke the ice.

"I'm not going anywhere. It was just a line." The accent was charming, and his smile fantastic. They both laughed.

"Margaret." She extended her hand.

"Freddy." He took her hand and kissed it with a slight bow.

"Do you come in here often?" He asked. It looked like he was going to continue giving her his line, but it was an old game, and she knew how to play it very well.

"I grew up with Nora, the owner. We went to school together. Her family has owned this place for three generations. Good food and friendly. Not real often, but maybe once a week."

"What brings you here?"

"I have work in the area. I move with the races. After Laurel, I go to Pimlico."

She began to gather her things and put her money on the bar. "Well, it was nice talking to you. Bye."

"I'll be here tomorrow same time," he volunteered.

Why would he think I'd come here tomorrow to see him, she wondered. Nothing memorable in this meeting except his honesty and that unbelievable smile that was still flashing like the Coors's beer neon above the bar.

Margaret decided to stop by A Street since it was on her way home. Maybe Grandma wouldn't be home, and a note would count as a visit. The door was locked, and knocking and calling did not bring Grandma. Margaret had to move two boxes to get the key under the mat. Snow White greeted Margaret and returned to the windowsill without acknowledging her or saying a word.

Margaret pulled the boxes from the porch and tipped them over to see who sent them. One was from the Middleburg Outfitters—Virginia's Premier Horse Country Shop. The smaller one was from Swiss Colony, marked perishable. "Oh Lordy. I wonder what all this means." She said to the boxes before writing a note for Grandma and replacing the key.

Grandma pulled her little Honda into the drive before Margaret made her get away.

"Hey, Sweety. Don't leave; I'm here."

Seeing Grandma was always a visual treat. Today she was dressed in polka dots. The full pink skirt with white dots swirled around her knees as she walked. The blouse was white with pink dots and had a large, embroidered collar. Her pink tennis shoes matched perfectly. It was quite possible that somewhere, she had a magic wand that would produce pixie dust. They went back into the house together.

"I've been line dancing at Blob's Park Biergarten. We had a bus trip from the Senior Center. Come on in. What would you like, dear, tea, Pepsi, or wine?" One thing Margaret was sure of –Grandma had never had wine to offer to anyone before.

"You've got wine?"

"Yes, I do. White or Red?" This was too good. Margaret hesitated, thinking over this proposition, as Grandma continued. "Let's see. I can offer you a fine ice wine from Niagara, Spanish Cava, which is a sparkling wine from the Piedmonts of Spain. Also, from France I have Condrieu, Pinot Noir, a vintage white. French Cabernet Sauvignon and Chardonnay are both well reputed. I also have Merlot from California."

"...What!?" Margaret's mind was blown.

"Now child, don't make me go over that again. Do you want red or white, dry or medium? Cava is the only sweet." Margaret had been to most of these wine regions across the globe, but she could not reconcile the choices here at Grandma's house, especially when she had just come from the best beer and burger place in Laurel.

"You know, Grandma. I think I'll skip the wine. Give me the Pepsi." Margaret slid into the new rocker.

Grandma came back with two Pepsis and a bag of chips.

"What a treat, Margaret," she remarked as she parked her red curls in the wing chair.

"What's new?" Margaret didn't know what else to say.

"I'm taking the wine appreciation course by the University of Maryland Extension Service. I have learned a lot. We are going to a vineyard in Western Maryland on Saturday."

"Where do you take the class?'

"At the High School on Montgomery Street. It is sponsored by the Senior Center. I can walk if the weather is good. Sarah wanted me to get involved there. One of her better ideas. I have met some nice people and made new friends." Margaret's interest was sparked, and she didn't want it to sound like an inquisition. But she had a lot of questions for Grandma. She drank her Pepsi and tried to decide which question would be most important.

"Do you drink wine?"

"I tried it. It was just as I remembered...nasty stuff." Margaret leaned back in the chair and relaxed. "So...my friends come here and drink it." Margaret sat up so fast that the rocker came forward and banged the back of her head with a crack.

"Goodness, Margaret. Looks like you broke something loose in that wonderful chair that Sarah got at Goodwill. Tish, tish!" The twinkle in her eye and voice belied her concern.

"What friends?"

"My friends from the class. We had a class trip to visit a liquor store to see the many wines. It seemed a shame not to buy from the nice man, and we couldn't take it back to the school grounds. Just seemed perfect to have our tasting here. I think I am the only one who didn't like the taste. Two had to spend the night." Margaret was on her feet.

"Dear, aren't you going to finish your Pepsi?"

"I have to go. When is your next class?"

"Tomorrow. It's just six classes. I think I know it all now. We have the graduation party Saturday. I thought a little imported cheese would be a nice touch." She pointed at the box from Swiss colony. "You know Margaret, I don't want to hurt Sarah's feelings, but I don't like that rocker. It puts me to sleep. Don't worry, you didn't break it, and I never sit in it."

Margaret kissed her cheek and started for her car. "Come back soon; don't wait until I'm gone." Margaret had never heard Grandma say anything like that before.

Better tell Sarah, she said to herself.

Snow White couldn't wait for Grandma to settle on the sofa and take her place on her lap. "You should not have said that," she began

"Said what?"

"*...after I'm gone.*" her cat answered.

"I know, you are right. You are always right," Grandma admitted.

"Margaret doesn't know about your trip. None of them do," Snow White reminded.

"I blew it. I keep looking for a time to tell them about Spain, but I can't seem to get a chance to tell them anything. My grandchildren are the busiest people in the world. I'm always surprised when they have a minute to stop by A Street and drink half a Pepsi and three potato chips."

"They need to learn a thing or two about slowing down," the cat purred.

"I'm trying. I'm trying," Grandma answered.

❧ ❧ ❧

Margaret approached Sarah's house looking for renegade kids. Sarah worked two days a week; she kept grandchildren every other day. Kids—constantly. Thank goodness the house and yard are large. Margaret never considered going there if it was raining. Today, there was a good chance that whatever kids were there would be outside but three were running through the kitchen.

Margaret peeked in and decided to abort her visit.

"I want to talk to you about my visit with Grandma this evening. Give me a call." She started backing out the door.

"Wait, Margaret. Come on in. We can talk now. I will turn on the TV for the kids."

"No. I'm going home and take an aroma bath. You can call me later." Margaret wanted a get-away.

"What's an aroma bath?" Sarah wanted to keep her sister.

"You know. Bubbles in the tub with scented candles and music in the room."

"You must be crazy. Why would you want to do that?"

"It is kind of like leaning on the front door after the grandchildren go home. You know, quiet and calm. And you just stand there for a delicious moment. Same feeling—just lasts a little longer in the bathtub." Sarah understood and reluctantly waved to her departing sister.

It was almost ten when Sarah called Margaret. She sounded so tired that Margaret hated telling her about Grandma's wine parties and parting words.

"It can wait. I'm ready for bed." Margaret tried to make light of it.

"Tell me," Sarah insisted. Sarah would not be put off; her innate desire to hold all the strings demanded Margaret's report. She insisted, no matter how tired she was or how late the hour. "What did you come by the house to tell me, Maggie?"

"I'll come for coffee tomorrow. It's too late to talk tonight. Good night, Sis."

That night, Margaret slept well after her aroma bath and wine. Sarah tossed and turned. Grandma drifted off peacefully with dreams from the book she had been reading—*Spain, the Magical Place.*

£ £ £

The next morning, coffee was barely poured when Sarah's questions started. "What did you want to tell me?"

Margaret had decided overnight not to tell Sarah about the wine party.

"Really, Sis. It was nothing. Do you have a muffin or donut to go with this coffee?" Trying to derail Sarah was futile.

"Maggie!" she demanded. "You wanted to talk about your visit with Grandma yesterday. Spill the beans!"

"Grandma joined a wine group sponsored by the Senior Center, and they had a meeting on A Street," Margaret spit it out—the taste of her message was bitter in her mouth.

"Who's in that wine group? How old were they? How many?" The expected questions flew.

Margaret didn't know enough to put Sarah at ease "I don't know." Her answer fueled Sarah's distress.

"The last meeting of the wine class is Saturday."

"A Street?"

"Yes, Grandma has cheese for refreshments. She will be fine with her Pepsi; she thinks wine is nasty. Relax Sis. I'll crash the meeting Saturday. I'll make an appearance and make sure it's ok."

"No, I'll go," Sarah asserted. "Tom will go with me if need be."

"I think I should go. I can imagine how excited Ted will be to go to his wife's grandmother's wine party. I'm goin'. That's that." Margaret insisted.

"I'm going, too. And I'm taking Ted. Suppose there is trouble? May need a man there." Sarah exerted her seniority and wisdom.

"For Christ's sake, Sarah. They are from the senior center. Probably all of 'em are over seventy years old . . . and 75% women. Old farts drinking wine. I'm sure unless Grandma drinks a glass, it isn't the first glass of wine those senior citizens had imbibed. I will not be part of a NATO alliance going to A Street to handle a raid on Grandma's digs." Margaret was angry. "Yes, stopping by to make sure everything is ok for Grandma is wise, but if you do it your way—go. Take your reinforcements. I'll be elsewhere. " Margaret got up to leave.

Sarah took Margaret's arm and pulled her back to the table. "I know we look at Grandma's situation differently. Sorry, Sis."

"I can't live in your constant emergencies. Lighten up." Margaret was on her last nerve.

"I'll try. I really will. After we get over this wine-drinking party, I'll lighten up." Sarah gave Margaret's hand a squeeze as a promise.

Then Margaret mentioned Grandma's remark— *when I'm gone.* Sarah went over the edge and forgot her promise to lighten up.

"Sis, it is not unusual for the older generation to refer to times when they won't be here." Margaret tried to insert reason and regretted continuing a conversation that included Grandma.

"Grandma is sick!" Sarah pronounced. Her alarms were activated. "Could be dying. We have to get her to Doc Belford." Sarah couldn't help being *Sarah.*

"I don't believe that. If she were sick, she would tell us." Margaret countered. Margaret eased her tone and continued. "Sarah, don't cry. It was a passing remark, almost a joke that Grandma would say to me and never, ever, say to you."

"This explains everything— the hair color, the crazy things, Don't you see? We have to get her to Dr. Belford and find out what's going on."

"No, I don't see."

Margaret knew it was out of her hands. The new, immediate, paramount mission to see Dr. Belford and get a diagnosis was clear and established in Sarah's mind.

"Dr. Belford will tell us how sick and how long she has." Once again, Sarah stood in her conviction. She threw it into the air, out the window, and through the hole that had not been cut in the wall yet.

Margaret drank her coffee down in two gulps and shook her head. Once again, Margaret walked out of Sarah's house without a soft, pleasant goodbye.

Chapter 6

John

John had a mission of his own to see for himself if Grandma really needed intervention. John was the oldest of the grandchildren. He decided the best way to live up to his position as the eldest was to stay away from his siblings. He never attended family meetings, refused to *pick cotton* with them, and made his own singular relationship with Grandma. His siblings thought he acted superior. John knew that, and he liked it.

The *Grandma problems* his brothers and sisters saw were of no interest to John. He did not know about the *crazies*, as Sarah called Grandma's actions of late. He did not know that Sarah thought the old gal was dying. You could say he was out of the loop. John liked it that way, too. This family could drive a person crazy. However, he did know about the meeting to talk about Grandma. Sarah called him and left a voicemail. Of course, he was tied up and could not take the call or make the meeting.

John and Pete were tall in this family of mostly short people—topping out at six feet. With the thick shock of hair, he appeared even taller. He was a loner but had not started out that way. Two failed marriages forced the issue. Relationships did not work for him and explaining them was even more impossible. John decided to live alone, to be alone, and to think as one. To say that his family did not understand him would be an understatement.

John gave up on marriage. He did not know if he was afraid of meeting and marrying another mismatch or of meeting and marrying the *right* woman. Deep inside, he hoped the *right* woman would find him. He spent time and money on himself—hair care from a salon in Baltimore. Finger and toenails buffed in a shop in Ellicott City—subscriptions to The Wall Street Journal and the National Symphony. John became beyond sharp in his dress; he was runway-worthy. Each shirt, jacket, or sweater was a perfectly coordinated choice. His belts were fine leather of uncounted shades of brown, black, and cordovan. His shoes were classic and stylish. When the ex-wife, who had alimony, died and his only child finished college, he spent that extra money improving his lifestyle. It was a generous bundle, almost like winning the lottery. He had no intention of spending it on another wife. When the *right* woman found handsome, well-dressed, sophisticated John Cotton, she would have her own money. He knew what he was doing.

Today, John decided to go see for himself what is going on with Grandma. He loved the old lady and felt she was the only woman he could trust. When he got there, a note was pinned on the door: "Be right back. Key under the mat." John unlocked the door, replaced the key (in case someone else came while he was waiting), went in, and relocked the door. He walked through the front room and kitchen, nonchalantly looking around. Nothing appeared to have changed except this new rocking chair and all these tour books and brochures spread across the table.

John sat in the rocker. Crash! It went to pieces, and John was dumped on the floor like a sack of potatoes. Instinctively he secured his toupee. He wanted to laugh, but it hurt too much. "Smart old cookie," he spoke aloud, "leaves the house open and sets booby traps." Then John realized he was hurt. He could not move. The pain was somewhere on his right side, groin, traveling down his leg. He used his arms to pull pieces of the chair from under his body, but even that was horrific. One of the rockers was causing pain in his left side. It took almost ten minutes to clear the debris from under his hurt body. John needed to rest and think, but the pain made thinking and decision-making impossible. Calling 911 was the only thing that came to mind. The telephone wire was within reach, and he began pulling it, causing things to fly off the secretary just behind him. The phone came along with the books, paper clips, and junk that was piled beside it. He dialed and managed to tell his predicament and location to the emergency operator.

"911. What is your emergency?"

"I've fallen and I can't get up." John was breathing heavily and could hardly speak.

"Are you injured?"

"Yes. Please ... Send help."

"Give me your location."

"2-o-something A Street. Laurel. I can't think ... Can't remember the number."

"Are you in the house?"

"Yes."

"Sir. Are you bleeding?"

"No, I don't think so."

"We are sending help. Try again. The house number?"

"Hell, I can't think of the number. My car is out front. Tag MD 435RB. Come quick."

"Stay on the line, sir. EMT is on its way." Exhausted by the pain and effort, he laid his head back and let the toupee fall like a tired rat on Grandma's carpet. He tried to breathe deeply, counting each breath to take his mind off the pain that was racing up and down from his hip. It was bad, very bad. So was the pain in his chest as it circled his body and made each breath a terror.

The sirens wailed, and the EMTs arrived and got to John very quickly. "Thanks for the note on the door," one quipped, "we found the key. And put it back." John would never have been able to unlock the door and let them in.

He was transported to the Greater Laurel Beltsville Hospital before Grandma returned from her lecture at the Senior Center. She would have loved to have a visit with John; he was always cheery and good for a laugh. If he had let her know he was coming, and she would have skipped the lecture—"The Broken Hip—Protect Yourself from Falls." As it was, she had no clue who had been in her house.

The smashed chair and desk items on the floor were a mystery. "Who's been sitting in my chair?" she wondered and said aloud, " ... and broke it all up! Must have been Goldie Locks." Grandma started picking up the rocker pieces, and when she lifted the seat, a rat jumped to the floor and startled her. The quick old lady lifted the floor lamp and, with a swift blow, killed it. Then she beat it to mutilation with the base of the lamp. Her heart was fluttering with the rush of adrenalin from the kill—one more blow for good measure. The weapon was bent and no longer stood erect. It would have to go out with the pieces of the rocker, the cushion, and the dead rat.

Out in the shed, Grandma found Irving's shovel and prepared to get the dead animal out of her living room and into the garden as soon as possible. She buried it and ran the shovel over the ground, smoothing it nicely. The pieces of rocker fit neatly into the trashcan and the lamp stood beside it to be picked up tomorrow—regular trash day.

Lucille was tired and needed a nice cup of tea to face the dilemma of writing a thank you note to Sarah for items that no longer existed. Sarah would have to understand. It did not matter who broke the chair. She believed in the old adage: *It would all come out in the wash.*

She went out and checked the mat to make sure the key was replaced, and it was. "Whoever came in the house knew how important that is," she told Snow White who had peeked out from the closet.

🐾 🐾 🐾

While this was happening to John, Sarah was in Dr. Belford's waiting room. The wait is always long, but when you do not have an appointment, it behooves Judy Adams, the receptionist, to make a point and keep you waiting longer. Sarah looked up when that same receptionist came to tell everyone waiting that Dr. Belford would not see anyone else today. "I'm sorry, but those waiting to see Dr. Belford will have to see Dr. Casey as Dr. Belford was called to the hospital. If you would rather reschedule, come to the window."

Sarah stepped to the window. "Dr. Casey cannot help me, Judy. Can I make an appointment for tomorrow, or could Dr. Belford call me at home? I need to talk to him about Grandma."

"You will have to bring your grandmother with you to discuss her medical issues. Dr. Belford cannot break confidentiality. That is unless you have a letter from her authorizing him to do so. A phone call won't work. You understand what I mean?"

"Yes, I see. I will call tomorrow after I talk to her and make sure she can come with me. Thanks Judy."

"By the way, Dr. Belford's call from the hospital was concerning your brother, John." Judy obviously vacated her obligation to patient confidentiality.

"He's at the hospital?"

"Yes. Just admitted."

Sarah was out in a flash. She suddenly had another family mission.

When she got to the hospital, Dr. Belford had already read the X-ray and called in an orthopedic surgeon. As they spoke, John was being readied for surgery. "Can I see him?" she asked.

"Of course." She was led into a curtained room where her brother looked older than he had in years. His fine clothes were rolled and stowed in a clear plastic bag under the gurney. John looked so old—like Dad when she saw him in his casket.

"John, what happened?" Her concern dripped all over her brother but thankfully, he was groggy, already under the effects of the sedative.

"I fell ... hip's broken." was all he could manage.

"I'll stay right here until you come out of surgery. Everything will be fine." Sarah patted his hand.

"Go ... get ... Harry ... Grandma's ... He drifted off as he was wheeled to the operating room.

"How sweet that he is still concerned about Grandma, and who in the world is Harry." Sarah said aloud to the empty corridor. She tried to call all her siblings but only got Margaret and Mark.

Margaret was the first to arrive, and Sarah took her aside. "John's in surgery to repair his hip. I don't know how it happened. Do you know who Harry is? John has been asking for Harry?" Sarah finished.

"Don't know any Harry. Do you think our John has sworn off women and gone to the other side? Come to think of it, I haven't seen John with a woman for the last three years, and for the previous twenty-five years, he was never without one! How about that!"

"Maggie! John? No, can't be. You're wrong.'"

"Wrong, hell! He asked for Harry, didn't he?"

"Yes, but he had had a shot for pain and was drifting off. Asked for Grandma, too."

"Dear, sweet sister. That stuff is like a truth serum. You don't lie when you are under the influence of those drugs. Harry and Grandma are probably the only people John cares about since his daughter married that redneck and took her expensive college degree to West, by God, Virginia."

"Gay! John?" Sarah was dumbfounded and at this crack in the perfection that was her family. Margaret loved it. John and Harry. Sounded like a London Insurance Company—*John and Harry, Ltd!* Or a fancy mail order house that can send a 6 oz. butter rum cake for $34.95 plus shipping.

"John and Harry," Margaret said aloud. She could not wait to meet Harry. It all fit now. John and his fancy clothes and new lifestyle. Surely, he had a closet full of clothes for cross-dressing too. What a hoot! She liked John more as a renegade than as the standoff, better-than-anyone-brother she had come to resent. John was coming back into the fold. He was flawed, and he fit much better now.

"I'll be the first in the family to accept them as a gay couple," she put in the air as her siblings began to arrive in the waiting room. "I think it's great."

Sarah needed to walk away. Needed a cigarette. She passed Mark as he arrived. "Doc Bedford's with John. An orthopedic surgeon was called in. He'll recover. That's all we need to think about." The first drag was delicious.

Mark went straight to the emergency nurses station, flashing his clergy badge. He learned that John had been transported from A Street by the Laurel Rescue Squad, information he immediately shared with his sisters.

"Broke his hip at Grandma's?" Sarah could not figure out how it happened. "In the house? Or on the sidewalk?" She mused.

"I'll bet he has a good story," Margaret could not wait to learn the details.

The surgery went fine and in two hours the surgeon came to tell Sarah, Margaret and Mark that John was resting comfortably with a hip replacement instead of a pin to repair it. His recovery would be swift, and rehabilitation would begin in the morning. They could see him as soon as he got to a regular room from the recovery area. Only one could go into recovery. Mark elected himself, as clergy, to do so.

"Hi, Bro. How you doing?" Mark greeted. John was groggy but managed a weak smile as Mark offered a short prayer.

"Cut the religious stuff. I need a favor?"

"Anything."

"Get my toupee from Grandma's front room" He was drifting. "And, Mark . . . " he whispered. "Whoever's out there . . . tell 'em to go home . . .please."

Meanwhile, Sarah secured Margaret's solemn promise not to tell the family about John and Harry. After all, that would be John's decision and had to be made without the influence of drugs.

Mark came from the recovery room with the report.

"John is sleeping. He did well. The news is that John wears a toupee, and without it, he looks just like Dad now. It seems it fell off in the accident, and the Laurel Rescue Squad transported him without it. He will be very disappointed if we don't find it. I talked to Jim. He's going to get Grandma and hopefully retrieve the toupee from her house."

"Can we go in to see him now," Sarah was anxious.

"He wants the toupee more than he wants to see you. In fact, He asked me to tell you all to go home. I'll wait for Jim and Grandma and turn them around."

"Fine with me. He's OK. Let's go." Margaret was out of there in time to get to Sam's for a beer by four o'clock and possibly see Freddy again.

Sarah's grandkids would be coming for dinner; she had to leave, but it wasn't easy, knowing John didn't mean her when he sent them away.

When Jim arrived with Grandma, Mark took the Lord's name in vain. "Jesus."

She had on riding pants, a red hunt jacket, black boots, and a bowler hat atop the red curls. He expected a tricolor hound to follow her into the hospital waiting room.

"Jim's waiting to come in. Said he would rather have me make a solo entrance. Whatever that means." Grandma advanced across the room. " How's John?"

Mark looked at his grandmother's wild dress and tried to stay focused. "Doin' good. I just saw him. No one can see him until he is moved to a room. John wants everyone to go home," he added. "They replaced his hip and taped his ribs. Three are fractured. Really, Grandma, you can come back tomorrow." Mark hoped he could redirect her.

Grandma ignored him, crossed the room, and mounted the arm of the sofa. He imagined her beating the sofa with her riding whip and galloping across the room. It was like being in a cartoon and trying to awaken himself, but this was real, and he needed to escape. Mark had just embraced his spiritual self and was about to have a secular breakdown. He wanted to shout, *Grandma what are you doing?* when he should be asking, *What Would Jesus Do?*

"Dear, these pants are stiff and hard to sit in. Please excuse me for choosing this seat. Would it be better if I stood?" She lifted her leg and threw it backward off the sofa as if she were dismounting a steed. Mark went to his knees—thinking he would have to catch her, but she maintained her balance saying, "Mark, get up. Don't be so obvious with your praying. Less display would be better."

"They have a room number for your brother, now," announced the volunteer—just in time. The tableau ended as Jim entered the room. "One visitor at a time. But I'll allow two for a short visit."

Jim turned on his heel. Mark and Grandma went in.

John was sitting up, drinking some water. Feeling better, he was delighted to see Mark and Grandma, and smiled as he took in her riding habit, possibly the sedatives helped a lot.

"Well, Grandma, that is quite a red jacket!"

Well," she responded, "that is quite a bald head!" John instinctively rubbed his hand across his head, missing his toupee very much. "Did you find my toupee in your front room?"

"No. I didn't know you wore one, and I didn't know you lost it in my front room. How would it get there?"

"I lost it when I fell and broke my hip."

"At my house?"

"Yes, Grandma. I sat in that rocker, and it gave way."

"Well, that explains a lot. I wondered who broke the chair. I didn't know you were hurt until Jim came to get me. Sorry I missed your visit. Don't worry about the chair."

"I am not worried about the chair; I'm worried about my hairpiece." John was getting agitated. "My very expensive hairpiece. Could you have thrown it out by mistake?"

"I don't think so. I will go back and look under everything. I did unpack and throw away some boxes my riding clothes came in today." She pinched the leg of her trousers to draw John's attention to her pants in case he hadn't noticed her outfit. "I threw all that packing away, but how could it have gotten mixed up in that?"

John was getting more frustrated by the minute. "Mark, have you got time to go with her to look for it?" John laid his bald head back on the pillow. "I'm feeling nauseous!"

"John, let me say, you don't need a toupee. I like you the way you are." Grandma said exactly what John did not want to hear.

The nurse passed them in the doorway, advising that the patient had had enough visitors for today. All John could do was nod in agreement. She fluffed his pillow and offered him water. John looked into her deep brown eyes and her pretty face with lots of smile lines. Then John checked her left hand for a ring. *Oh, no. No ring.* He thought as he drifted off to an exhausted sleep still laced with medication.

Grandma went to the bed, kissed John's check, and left in a slow gallop.

Chapter 7

Mark

Mark had the pleasure of walking Grandma through the hospital lobby. As if her bright curls, red jacket and riding pants were not causing enough attention, she was slapping her thigh with the riding whip with each step. Whop! Whop! "I'll carry that for you Grandma," he said as he reached for it. She slapped his hand with the whip. Mark let out a yelp. He reacted by grabbing the whip and found himself struggling with her for possession of it.

"Stop it, Scampy," Grandma resorted to his childhood nickname. It only took a few seconds to end this little tug of war, but when Mark let go, Grandma waved the whip in the air, and people in the lobby gave out a cheer. Mark's hand went up to his cleric's collar. Embarrassment beyond measure colored his face and neck. Grandma kept walking. Mark ran to catch up with her.

At the door the valet said to Grandma, "Are You ok, Ma'am? Need me to call security?"

"No, thank you," she responded. "He's harmless."

The ride to A Street was quiet, but when they got there, Grandma knew she needed to have some time with Mark to mend fences. He parked the car in the rear and followed her to the door, staying clear of her whip. "Come in, sweetheart?" she asked brightly, and as he started to decline, she went to another tactic. "I need a prayer." He could not refuse this. Mark knew she did need a prayer and was glad she realized it, too. "I will put on some tea unless you would enjoy a glass of wine."

He could really use a drink. "Wine?"

"Yes," she said. 'I have red or white."

"Red is better for you. Do you have Merlot?" A nice big water glass of Merlot was set before him.

"I don't have wine glasses. Hope you don't mind." Mark did not mind; he was still dealing with the fact that she had wine. He took a taste and found that he had a reservoir of delicious Merlot of fine quality. He walked to the front room, sat in Grandpa's chair, and relaxed for the first time in about twelve hours.

"I'll be back in a minute, Mark. I'm gonna get out of these clothes."

Mark thought that was the second good idea she had had since they arrived, so he leaned back, sipped his wine, and let his mind go back to days in this house when they were all children. The table was stretched to the limit. Mark was the youngest boy and he and Margaret, the two youngest, were allowed to eat at the coffee table, sitting Indian fashion on the floor. They got a reward if they did not spill anything while doing so. Margaret did not care about the reward, but Mark did, and it was a joint venture. Mom was not going to get into a battle about who spilled and who did not. They had to work together to keep food and drink off the carpet. Margaret would load her fork and make big circles overhead on a path to her mouth and Mark would pray, "God, don't let it spill." His earliest remembered prayer.

🦢 🦢 🦢

Grandma came back in her new yellow fuzzy robe and orange slippers. Her hair had been fluffed up, and she had a purple headband with small purple bows across it. He thought she looked like Tweedy Bird or maybe a fruit bowl filled with oranges, bananas, and grapes. The wine was mellowing. He smiled at the bright joy she brought to the room. He rose from Grandpa's chair and gave her a big hug, "I love you, Grandma."

"I love you, too, dear." She brought her tea and the wine bottle to join him. The wine was really good, so Mark poured more while she went to get some food. Neither one had eaten since lunch. Peanut butter and jelly was his favorite and should go well with the wine, especially since she had grape jelly. It tasted good to Grandma, and Mark was at the point where everything was good with him.

"Should we pray now?" he asked, slightly slurring his words.

"Yes, let's get that out of the way," Grandma agreed.

Mark raised his eyebrow at that remark, but his rosy outlook allowed it to pass as Grandma emptied the bottle in his glass. Mark took another drink and asked, "Shall we stand or sit for the prayer?"

"Let's sit this time; we'll stand the next time."

"Good idee!" He took another swallow, bowed his head, and

nodded off. Grandma cleared her throat, and he began to pray. "We are gathered here . . . in this place . . . where all blessings flow . . .holding these truths to be self-evident . . . while the dew is still on the roses . . . indibisable . . . on the wings of a snow white dove . . . in God we trush. Amen."

Grandma easily led him to the sofa and covered him with his favorite quilt from her collection. She stuffed a soft pillow under his head as she gently unfastened and removed the stiff white collar. She kissed his forehead and headed upstairs to her bath, singing 'When the Roll is Called Up Yonder.'

Snow White gingerly crept from the closet. "I'm so glad to see you," she purred and spoke. "It has been a harrowing day. I wasn't sure that was you downstairs now."

"Snow, did you see John come in today?" She asked the cat.

"I heard someone downstairs, but before I came down, a loud crash sent me back up. It was a terrible afternoon. A crash and then sirens. You know me—scaredy cat. Lots of strangers coming into the house. Maybe you should have a dog instead of me. I let strangers in, and I'm frightened of sirens." She paused to stretch., "I'm glad to see you," Snow added, obviously still traumatized.

"I'm sorry you got frightened. John broke the rocker and his hip. He had surgery an hour ago. Will be alright, though." Grandma took Snow in her arms to offer comfort. "Mark's here now. He's downstairs, sleeping.

"I really like Mark. He is so gentle when he speaks to me. Very sincere and caring," the cat responded.

"I agree, but he hasn't settled into his religious role very well. Too tense. I wanted to talk to you about Mark. This might be a good time." Grandma started the conversation while getting in the tub. Snow took her perch on the toilet seat. "You have such good instincts," Grandma complimented

"Thank you," Snow purred.

"Mark might be the grandchild to listen to me. Maybe he can understand and tell the rest of them to let me manage my own life."

"I'm glad you realize what's happening here, but I doubt Mark will be much help," Snow White answered frankly. "Mark's career and high-security clearances tended to make him resistant to open discussions. Besides, since he retired and became a deacon, he's confused. Not that sure about things," she added.

Grandma smiled her agreement and finished her bath.

£ £ £

It was nearly nine o'clock when Mark stirred from his long nap. Grandma was sitting in the wing chair, alternately thinking of this grandson and reading Down Under on a Dime. She had the book across her lap and was holding Mark's collar in her left hand. Mark was definitely the most complicated of them all, and she found it hard to discount some of his unusual behavior as she could the rest of them. How could a man build a career as a spy and suddenly become an ordained clergy? She loved telling her friends that her grandson was like James Bond. Now it wasn't as exciting to say he was the new Billy Graham.

All those years at the super-secret National Security Agency had provided a good life for Mark and his family and some exotic travels for Mark. He had been around the world many times and even spent a three-year tour in Germany. The family tried to get him to tell what he knew, but he always told them they *didn't have the need to know.* His lips were sealed as if by super glue or, as she said, super-secret-agency-glue. World events often kept Mark at his office for long hours, but he could not even be coaxed to comment on what the Washington Post published in its headlines. It was a mystery what he did, but he turned to God a few years ago, and she figured his work must have led him to embrace the religious life. Grandma really had not been fair to him, taking his new avocation so lightly—none of the family had. She had always let God find her and never saw the need to go looking for Him. Now, she had a treasured grandson walking with this advertisement around his neck. She looked at the collar; she even put it around her own neck and removed it quickly as if it might lock on and never come off.

Mark rolled over and looked at Grandma. "How long have I been sleeping?"

"Oh, almost three hours."

"What are you doing with my collar, Grandma?"

"Just holding it. Here." She reached out to give it back. He took it but did not put it on. Instead, he twirled it on his finger much as she had done, then he stuffed it in his shirt pocket and got up. His head hurt and he had a burning thirst and was hungry again. He decided on ice water Campbell's soup, saltines, and butter. Grandma told Mark about her wine class but left out the part about her friends drinking the wine at her house. That upset Margaret and no use in upsetting the family clergy, too.

"I wondered how you picked such a good Merlot," was his only comment.

"Let's call the hospital and make sure John is doing OK." The call was made, and the nurse on duty said John wanted to talk to Mark if he called. She went to see if he was awake and sure enough, John came on the line.

"Hi, Mark. I was waiting to see if you found my toupee."

"I forgot . . . but I am at Grandma's now, and if it is here, we will find it."

"Oh, it's there all right. Just bring it in the morning."

"Sure. How is it going?"

"Good, I guess. They'll have me walking tomorrow. Right now, I am feeling no pain."

"How come you aren't asleep?"

"This nurse goes off in an hour. I'll sleep after she is gone." That seemed a little weird to Mark, but he let it go. It was good to hear his brother's voice, which sounded strong and normal. All John is worried about is that toupee.

"Grandma, he wants us to look for his toupee. Do you know where he fell?"

"Right here in this room. I found the broken chair that threw him on the floor here by the window. I cleaned and swept. The trash is in the cans, but I don't think you will find anything. I would remember a toupee."

Grandma went down on all fours. She was a little yellow beetle or Volkswagen scooting around the floor. Her orange slippers were taillights as she was peeking under chairs and sofa. Mark did the same and looked in the same places as she, finding nothing. They were like carnival bumper cars, forward, back, and reversing whenever they touched each other. Grandma even honked her imaginary horn, but Mark took the job more seriously. John's toupee was not in this room. They had no choice; they had to go through the trash. By now, it was close to eleven, the wind was blowing, and they needed a flashlight. Mark moved the lamp and shovel that were propped against the cans and dragged the containers over to the steps where the porch light and Grandma, in her yellow robe, was competing with the moon to light the area.

"You do that one, I'll do this," Mark directed

"God, I hope we find it quickly. These cans are stuffed." They began emptying the contents on the ground piece by piece. Grandma had the can with chair parts in it and Mark had the one with packing material from the western wear company. She took each piece of the chair out and looked to see if John's toupee was snagged, waiting to be rescued. The pile on the ground was growing, and she was reaching deeper into the can. Meanwhile, Mark had a pile of bubble wrap and filler paper beside his can when a gust of wind sent it scurrying across the back lawn. He chased it down, throwing his foot out to stop it while he reached to grab it before the wind took it further. A muffled scream came from Grandma back at the porch. Mark turned to run back and saw her knees and feet kicking in the air from the other can. Before he could get to her, the can tipped over, and Grandma, in the can, rolled down the incline of the back ally. He grabbed the shovel and ran for Grandma, who was screaming bloody murder, which sounded like a yodel as the can went round and round in a slow roll. Mark got in front of the rolling dervish and set the shovel between himself and the can full of Grandma. The can hit the shovel. The ride was over. The shovel saved Grandma from rolling onto Main Street and Mark's shins from damage. He was almost afraid to pull her out, but he did, very gently. He carried her back, laid her on the pile of bubble wrap and packing paper and knelt beside her. "Are you alright, Grandma?" He was shaken and near tears.

"I am," she said. "Thank God I had just taken hold of the chair cushion when over I went. I held it around my head." *God is so good*, was Mark's thought.

"I think you will be sore and bruised. Just lay here a moment don't move while I get this mess back together. John's toupee is not here. I'm glad this shovel was here."

"I had it out to bury the rat I killed in the front room to-day." It had not dawned on Grandma, but the light came on for Mark. There couldn't be a rat in Grandma's house. And she could never catch and kill one if it was there.

"Rat?'

"Yes, under the broken chair. One whack with the lamp and he was done. I buried him in the garden over there." She pointed.

Mark took the flashlight and found the place where the ground appeared recently smoothed over. He had lifted one scoop of dirt when three police cars arrived. One out front, one coming up the alley and one coming down the alley. The back of A Street was lit by their headlights and spotlights. Doors flew open and uniform men had Mark on the ground in hand-cuffs while another officer was checking Grandma for signs of life. The ambulance arrived in two minutes and thirty seconds.

Grandma enjoyed the attention, insisting she was only bruised and that the cushion did not cut off her breathing. She did not understand why the officer took the cushion as evidence. The shovel was taken with rubber gloves as evidence, too. None of the police officers knew Mark or even the Cotton family. And for the first time, the influx of new people into the small town affected Mark. "This can all be straightened out. You must be new in Laurel." He suggested, trying to be friendly.

"We aren't here to talk about us," the officer barked. Then he frisked him and held his head while Mark bent into the patrol car. At the station, the officer reported, "No wallet; no ID." Mark instinctively tried to reach for his wallet, but handcuffs jerked him straight. He remembered putting it on Grandma's coffee table before he went to sleep.

Mark was in a cell before Grandma got to Laurel Beltsville Regional Hospital emergency room. She kept asking them to bring in her son Mark, but, as usual, no one listened to Lucille Cotton.

"Mrs. Cotton, who will be with you here in the Emergency Room?' The duty nurse asked.

"My son, Mark," she replied.

The nurse knew the family and went to the phone book to look for Mark Cotton's number but there was no answer. Grandma was given a sedative. Before she drifted off to sleep, she told them that her grandson John was a patient in the hospital. Maybe she could see him.

🐜 🐜 🐜

Mark was not doing well at the police station.
"Ok, buddy, we are ready to talk to you now."

A police officer without a uniform was talking and Mark looked behind him to see who he was talking to but there was no one else in the cell. "Me?"

"We have a smart one here."

Mark was taken to a room with a desk and two chairs, where he was given the Miranda speech.

"OK. Let's begin." The officer had some forms and wanted

his name and personal information. He laughed when Mark listed his occupation as clergy. "Sure. Sure." Mark lifted his hand to his throat and felt that his collar was not in its place. He reached into the shirt pocket, and it was not there either.

"Tell us about the old lady."

"My grandmother. She and . . .

"Just answer the questions. How did she get hurt?'

"She went headfirst in the trash can. I wanted to . . .

"You put her in the trash can?"

"No. She fell in. I wanted to . . .

"Look, Bud, I said; just answer the questions. What about the cushion?"

"It was over her head. That was a good thing otherwise . . .A dirty look shut Mark down again. The questions were coming so fast. He realized he was not getting any of the facts through to this cop.

"What were you digging with the shovel?"

"I want to talk to my attorney, Peter Cotton."

"Ok. Brad, get this guy a phone. You can call now or in the morning."

"I'll call now." The officers left the room and let Mark call his brother in private.

"Pete. I know it is late, but I need help."

"At 12:15? This is unbelievable! Can it wait until morning?"

"I think they will keep me in jail if you don't come help me now."

" Good God. I just got a call from John in the hospital telling me Grandma is in the emergency room with cuts and bruises from someone breaking into the house. I was ready to leave for the hospital. Are you in the Laurel jail?'

"I am in the Laurel jail because they think I did that to Grandma?"

"Did you?"

"Christ, Pete. Not you, too! Nobody lets me talk. Grandma is not seriously hurt. I checked her myself before the police arrived. The neighbors must have called the police when they heard her screaming."

"Maybe you need to stay in the jail."

"Stop it! I tell you Grandma is fine. You know I wouldn't hurt her. Come down here and get me out so we can straighten this all out."

Pete took a moment to collect his thoughts. He was not a jailhouse lawyer but someone in the family needed help, and he wasn't sure if it was Grandma or Mark.

"I am going by the hospital and check on Grandma and then I'll come to the jail. Try to stay calm. I don't know what is going on, but this sounds like it will be one of the Cotton Pickin' Cotton's all-time best stories. I'll be there as soon as I can."

"Thanks." Mark's reply was laced with sarcasm. Actually, it was two hours before Pete and Grandma arrived at the jail to straighten everything out. She did not need to be admitted to the hospital as she had a scratch on her left elbow and bruises on her shoulders and hips. Nothing broken. She was a little tipsy from the medication, but Pete had to bring her into the station; he couldn't leave her in the car alone. It wasn't a pretty site. Her hair was like a copper Brillo pad; her yellow fuzzy robe was matted and soiled. Her oversized slippers that looked like oranges were torn and she had a tiny Band-Aid across the tip of her nose. She was a Raggedy Ann that had been more abused than loved. Pete led her to a chair in the empty anteroom and

went back to rescue his brother. Her head slumped over and she began to snore loud enough to interfere with the dispatcher, working at the desk in the next room.

"Hey Granny. Why are you here?" asked a police officer passing through the room.

"I am waiting to be taken home."

"Where's home?"

"206 A Street."

"Hey Bart! I'm going to take this lady to A Street. Unless you have a call for me."

"Nah, go ahead."

Grandma was home in bed while this last confusion was being solved at the police station. When she turned up missing, Pete went looking for answers from the dispatcher; Mark almost hoped that she would never be found.

The next day, John called his brother Jim to ask him to go over to dig up the muddy, mutilated hairpiece. When he asked Mark to go back for it, Mark said, "Go to Hell."

Chapter 8

Jim

J im missed all the hospital and jail nonsense, as usual. He managed to be somewhere else at the crazy times but stayed sympathetic to his family's real needs. Jim had the utmost respect for Grandma. He would gladly support her, her outlandish clothes, and wild plans. After all, it was well known in the family that Grandma had many special talents that she had put aside for this family. If she wanted to go for the gold now, it was all right with Jim. He would do all he could to take care of her, but if it meant keeping her down, Jim would draw the line. He decided to stop by Sarah's and gently suggest she *bug off.* It was probably a waste of time, but he would give it a try.

Sarah was feeding two grandchildren, one husband, two dogs, one cat and making a casserole for one sick neighbor. "Hey, Jim. Marge just called here looking for you! Give her a call before you come into the kitchen."

"I just talked to her on the cell."

"Good. Come on in and have some bar-b-que." He ate and

waited until only he and Sarah were left in the kitchen. "How is John?"

"He's doing well. I took Grandma to the hospital and only stayed a minute. A friend is picking her up to take her to whatever is her next event. "

"What can I do to keep you from worrying so much about her? She seems busy and happy. So, she wants to ride a horse. So what?" He decided not to tell Sarah about Grandma's attire when he dropped her at the hospital.

"It is so much more than that Jim. I think she sick, dying . . . Tears always affected Jim. " . . . doesn't have much time left. She told Margaret she didn't have much time at all."

Jim put his arm across Sarah's shoulder and pulled a tissue from the box. She dabbed and sniffed and continued.

"I went see Dr. Belford to ask about Grandma but Judy, you know, Doc's receptionist, said he couldn't talk to me about Grandma unless Grandma came with me. I think she is doing these dangerous things—trapeze, horseback riding—because ... because . . . " Sarah was seriously crying now.

"Sarah, if Grandma doesn't want to talk about her health, we have to honor that." Now the sobbing required more tissues and inquisitive peeks from a granddaughter in the next room.

"She looked the picture of health when I left her ten minutes ago and if she wants to ride a horse, good for her."

"We have to know in case she needs some treatments she is ignoring. I have to know!" Sarah was beginning to act frantic. Jim, who had always been sensitive to Sarah, felt her concern and decided that he needed to help Sarah more than Grandma.

"OK, Sarah. I'll tell you what. I will take Grandma to Doc Belford and see what is going on . . .but I warn you. I am not going along with anything that will clip her wings. In fact, if she has something terminal, I will encourage and help her do whatever she wants to do in the time she has. Now make me a cup of coffee and dry those tears."

Giving Sarah a job was the only immediate solution.

Jim tried to call Grandma but as usual, she was not home. Finally, he went by the house and left a note on the table for her to call him. He put the key back under the mat and headed home. His phone was ringing when he arrived. "I'll get it." He yelled, but the house was empty.

"Hi Grandma. How ya doin'?"

"I'm fine Jim. Been busy. Fredrico took me up to the riding stables on Gorman Road. They have a senior program on Tuesday afternoons. Gentle horses and nice people. We have been studying video tapes and getting to know the horses. This was my first time riding, and it was great. Although, I must say' it is hard on . . . you know, sitting and bouncing ..."

"Hard on the arse, Grandma?"

"You got it! I've got a tape, and I am to practice at home."

"How do you practice horse riding at home?"

"Well, it's like this. You put on the tape, which has a rider bouncing up and down with the horse's gait. You have to get on a proper seat and ride with the tape."

"A proper seat?"

"It can be a kitchen chair, straddling with the back between your legs, or it can be on the arm of a sofa. The important thing is to get the rhythm of the horse. It would be best if someone

would come and get on their knees on the floor and let me ride like you kids used to do with Grandpa. I suppose I could ask Fredrico to do that. I'd rather ask you." This visual was almost more than Jim could stand. He was trying to remember what he had called her for . . . must have been something.

"Don't call him. I'll be right over." Jim failed to give her credit for a sense of humor.

"Don't be ridiculous. I was only kidding." Grandma was agitated. "Did you really think . . . ", She hung up on him.

Jim had to go to see Grandma and apologize. *Sarah's makin' me crazy,* he thought. When he got there, she had forgotten about riding a horse and was at the table looking at two books Sarah had brought her: *Down Under on a Dime* and *Magical Spain.* She greeted her grandson with a big smile; so glad to see him.

"Sorry," Jim started an apology.

"No need," she replied. "I know I am doing things I haven't done before. I am taking riding lessons with Fredrico. And I don't need anyone's permission. If I did, who would that be? I take good care of myself. Give me a little credit. I have a brain. I can dress outlandishly and make people smile, and I can make a joke or two." Grandma made her point.

The smile in her chatter and a bear hug made everything right and Jim was reminded of the love and admiration he had had for this lady all of his life.

"We dressed up for a class picture this week. The stable had plenty of riding outfits, but they were all too big for me. I bought my own and had it on when I went to the hospital. I kinda like showing off," she laughed.

"You know something funny? I know each of my grandchildren's favorite things. You — Corvettes. Pete — Golf.

Sarah—James Garner. On and on. But none of you ever knew I loved horses. I loved Dale Evans, Roy Rogers, and Trigger. I always rode the horse on the merry-go-round. I have a picture of the ponies of Chincoteague Island in our bedroom. I have scarves and jewelry with horses and horseshoes." Grandma drew a breath. "No on noticed. And now, I'm learning to ride a horse."

"I love you, Grandma." A kiss on the cheek made them both happy.

The mission he accepted from Sarah gained new importance. Jim wanted Grandma to be in Dr. Belford's hands to ensure she is well enough to do all the things she wants to do in whatever time she has. Although he was not convinced that admiring horses, and riding horses, was the same thing at age 82. He went right to the point, hoping to avoid any further talk about horses.

"Grandma I would like for you to come with me to see Dr. Belford. When can I make an appointment?"

Jim. Sick? She thought. Immediately Grandma became concerned and wondered what Jim's health problems were. *Must be something serious and something he is keeping from Marge and his kids.*

"Sure. Let's see. I bowl Monday morning and have Red Hats at lunchtime, go riding Tuesday afternoon, Wine Club Wednesday, including lunch and go at the 'Y' on Fridays—no particular time." Since Jim was self-employed and not really that tied up; he could work around her schedule.

"I will call for Monday after your lunch. Where's the phone under all this mess?" She dug under the papers on the table and came up with the phone.

Jim made an appointment for Monday. He kissed Grandma's cheek and managed to get out of the house without discussing

horseback riding again. In fact, he scurried out without noticing what she was working on at the table. In his haste, Jim
set the phone down on top of the travel brochure for a senior
group tour of Spain. Like his brothers and sisters, Jim felt he
had escaped something by getting out of the door on A Street.
Something vague … *something* that he didn't have to think
about again until Monday.

Grandma was preoccupied with concern over Jim's health
and the bizarre request that she accompany him to the doctor.
She and Jim were often on the same wavelength, and he was the
least complicated of her grandchildren.

"Snow White! Where are you?" she called.

The cat slowly moved toward the calling voice. "Right here,"
Snow replied as she emerged from the drapes. "You know I
avoid Jim. The way he tries to scratch my ear like a dog," disgust
filtered through her words.

"Jim is gone."

"Did you tell him about Spain?"

"He left so quickly that I did not get a chance to tell him."

"Lucille, This happens all the time. Especially now that your
grandchildren are adult and have stopped listening to you. I see
them come in always with some mysterious agenda."

"I know, and I always think they are going to stay for a while.
Maybe have a glass of tea."

"They come through that door, preparing to leave. I have to
be careful I don't get stepped on." Snow white's attitude swept
down her humped back.

"Like Jim today. Gone before I had a chance to tell him what
I wanted to," Grandma lamented.

"They don't come to listen." Snow White spoke her mind.

"You're so smart; what do they come for? Goodness knows

this week has been a parade." Grandma paused. "All because of that crazy ride on a trapeze? Maybe I shoulda climbed that ladder years ago."

"They come to make sure you don't do anything to interrupt their busy lives," Snow spoke frankly.

Grandma got a cup of tea and sat wistfully at the table. The cat climbed on her chair cushion.

"Wouldn't you think **one** of them would want to know about **my** life?" Grandma asked the cat.

"Really?" Snow White stood up, weary of Grandma. "They think you have already had your life." Snow White was finished with this conversation. She hopped down and left the room.

♛ ♛ ♛

Monday Grandma was ready for Jim, still wearing her Red Hat regalia from lunch at Tag's Restaurant. Her purple pantsuit with the embroidered teapot on the front and little red hats around the neck was beautiful, especially with the plumbed hat of red feathers perched on her head. Club earrings, plus red jeweled shoes that she found in the costume department at Target (Dorothy in the *Wizard of Oz*) finished Grandma's look. Jim loved it and hopped out of the car, drinking his ever-present Coke Cola to give her a deep bow and open the door. He came in one of his Corvette's and she folded herself into the front seat inches above the roadway. Grandma loved every minute of the ride, especially the way Jim took the corner and threw the gearshift as if he were at Talladega. He smiled at her because he knew she loved riding in this car, whereas his siblings didn't. Too jealous.

"Too bad it is such a short ride to Doc's office." She lamented. "I usually walk here for my appointments." They arrived in 2 minutes and 35 seconds . . . almost like riding in a Kansas tornado. It was a little harder to unfold and get out of the car, especially being careful not to break any feathers on her hat.

"I went in to see Doc last Thursday. I wanted a complete check-up." She said as they sat in the waiting room. Jim nodded. As Judy opened the door and called "Jim and Lucille Cotton." They stood, and Grandma continued. "If only I didn't have arthritis."

Jim had a *What am I here for?* look on his face. In a nano-second Jim realized he was the only one who thought Grandma was the patient. Not Judy. Not Doctor Belford. And not Grandma. Two Cottons were there for an appointment that obviously was not for Grandma. Jim became enraged at Sarah for causing this predicament and he was incapable of redirecting.

"Good morning, Lucy, Jim. What can I do for you today?" Dr. Belford invited them in. "It looks like you are dressed for Red Hats today, Lucille."

"Doc, " Jim addressed the old friend of the family who had taken care of the Cottons for years. "Did Grandma get a clean bill of health recently?'

"I wish all my senior citizens took as good care of themselves." He squeezed her shoulder.

"Who is this appointment for?" Doc asked. Grandma pointed to Jim, who had to think quickly. "Doc, I need a clean bill of health. I thought you could check me out and Grandma could help with family history. She loves to ride in my Corvette. So here we are." It was lame, but Grandma smiled. Doc Belford raised his eyebrow and thought he had heard everything, but this was the first time a grown man brought his grandmother with him.

Jim felt like the fool he was.

"I tell you what. Lucy, you go to the waiting room and fill out some family history while I begin this checkup and schedule some tests." Lucille patted her grandson's hand and did as the doctor asked.

"Doc, I don't know why we are taking your time. So foolish. I brought Grandma here because Sarah said she had some terminal illness. Judy said you couldn't tell me anything about her without her coming too."

The doctor began to laugh. "Well, that explains a lot. Couldn't figure out what was going on. I assure you, your grandmother has a good handle on her health. She wanted a checkup because of that trip she is thinking about taking. I gave her all the support I could."

"Oh, my God. You have broken the confidence of your patient. We don't know anything about a trip." Jim replied.

"I'm not about to talk to you about your Grandmother's health, but I agree and as her friend, the family needs to know her travel plans. Maybe she hasn't had a chance to tell you. I'm sure checking with me was preliminary to making them. It was just a few days ago that she came in. Give your Grandmother time to decide what she wants. Meanwhile, try to keep Sarah calm. That is not easy. Before you leave here today, I will tell her she needs to get you kids clued in. Now, Jim, it has been a long time since you have been in. I see in your records I haven't seen you since you banged yourself up in that fast car about four years ago. Have you been going to another doctor?"

"Haven't needed to. Been fine."

"Let me check your vitals and draw some blood. You are going to pay for an office visit anyway."

The doctor did his thing—poking and listening, saying 'Mmmm" occasionally. The nurse took John's blood pressure, drew some blood, and took the blood pressure again. It was very difficult when the nurse, younger than his daughter, asked him to pee in a cup, which he wanted to refuse, but the cup was in his hand. Might as well—had to go anyway.

"The bathroom is right next door. I'll meet with you back here. Put your shirt on and leave the specimen there."

It was easier to call it a specimen and not have to hand it back to a teenybopper. John continued to do as he was told and waited for Doc Belford to return.

The door opened—it was Grandma. "What is taking so long? Is something wrong, Jim?"

"Nope. Doctors keep you waiting so you will be happy to see them come back into the room."

"I've got to get home soon."

"I'm sure it won't be long now." She smiled and closed the door.

Doctor Belford came back with a stack of prescriptions in his hand. "Well, Jim. It is a good thing you came in today. Your blood pressure is high, too high—180 over 98. We are going to start you on medication today, in fact, two medications.

"Are you sure?"

"I'm sure. We took it twice. We need an electrocardiogram and stress test. We scheduled them over at the outpatient lab in the hospital tomorrow. Is 11:30 good for you?"

"Yeah." Jim really wasn't computing this.

"Now, about your blood sugar. I didn't like what we got in your urine sample.

Whaa . . . what?"

"You need a fasting blood test. We will do that here before you go over to the hospital in the morning. No coffee; nothing except one of each of these medications. I'll have all your results tomorrow afternoon. Blood work here early. Hospital outpatient 11:30; here at 2:00 in the afternoon. I'll have Judy write this all down for you. Here are your prescriptions." He put some foil-wrapped pills in Jim's hand. "Take these samples and begin the blood pressure medicine now. Here is a cup of water. Get the prescriptions filled, and be sure to take them again in the morning before going for your tests. We don't want a stroke, do we?" That got Jim's attention. He didn't try to speak, he just nodded his head. The doctor could see that Jim was overwhelmed.

"Now, Jim. This is all manageable. You take your medications, and we will control these problems. Please repeat to me everything I have asked you to do."

"Take two now and two in the morning. Fill the prescriptions. Here in the morning for blood. Outpatient clinic and here at 2:00. Please, tell me that is all."

"Fasting. We will have to wait for the blood work. Eat light before your stress tests and lunch before you come here."

"Thanks, Doc . . . I think . . .

"Have a good day!" When Jim finally got to the waiting room, it was empty. Judy spoke up. "Your grandmother went on home; she didn't want to miss Oprah. She said it was about the new middle age, forty plus forty."

Great! He really didn't want to tell his 82-year-old grandmother, who didn't need prescriptions and tests, that he was a physical wreck.

£ £ £

Jim did as Doc Belford ordered; took his pills and went for the early tests where another sweet young thing required peeing in a cup and handled him discreetly. This test was more complex, with several blood tests and several small snacks. The results would be ready for Dr. Belford this afternoon. The sweet young thing gave him some crackers to eat, but he stuffed them in his pocket instead and headed to the hospital for the stress test.

Jim wished he had time for a cheeseburger at Sam's, but everything was taking longer and running late. He barely had time to get back to Dr. Belford's office by 1:50.

Grandma was waiting for him, dressed for her riding lesson but not the full *to the hounds* outfit. Today it was jeans, boots and plaid flannel. The handsome man sitting next to her was dressed identically. Jeans, boots, and an almost matching plaid flannel shirt. They looked like salt and pepper shakers made in Occupied Japan.

"Hi, Jim. I thought you might still want me with you for this appointment, too." It was never explained why Jim wanted her with him yesterday so it seemed logical that the reason might still apply today.

It had been a long, tiring morning. He was worn out, hungry, and lightheaded. This sight of Grandma and her riding instructor in matching outfits probably had nothing to do with it but, he fainted. It was a good place to pass out; help was immediate. Dr. Belford was quick to bring him around but would not let him get up. He was still trying when the paramedics arrived and began taking vitals and preparing him for the run to the hospital.

"What did you eat today?"

"Didn't have time to eat." Jim was drinking orange juice as he was carried to the ambulance . . . protesting all the way. He had just enough time to tell Grandma to call Marge. "Tell her where I am!" He was transported to Greater Laurel Beltsville Hospital as Dr. Belford called the emergency room to explain his condition and gave directions to admit him for cardiac and sugar monitoring.

Grandma told Fredrico "Mia Casa." There would be no riding lesson today and she had practiced with the tape until she was sure she could ride without getting a sore ass. Life is a challenge when you have grandchildren. She was not going to the hospital in riding clothes again today; she had to change first.

"These children are going to drive me crazy!" she told Snow White as she rushed to change outfits.

At the emergency room, someone said "Another Cotton? We have more here than the fields of Mississippi."

Jim gave up; he didn't fight or argue. The juice had made him feel fine but if they wanted to poke and prod, it was okay as long as they didn't want to cut. In fact, the only thing he said to those trying to take vitals and start an EKG was, "Whatever."

Three hours later Dr. Belford and Grandma walked into Jim's room. *Oh God, it must be bad news if Doc and Grandma have to come here together. And Grandma just looks like Grandma. No fancy clothes. No sparkles. Really bad news.* He was prepared to die.

"You are OK to go home, son. Good news and bad news. Which first?" The doctor asked.

"Good news! Please." Jim recovered from his doom's day revelry.

"Your heart checked out fine, both this morning on the stress test and this afternoon on the EKG."

"That is a relief. Thank you, Doc." He took two deep breaths and asked, "What's the bad news?"

" You have hypoglycemia, which means your body doesn't regulate your sugar intake very well and when you don't eat or drink your favorite soda, your sugar bounces up and down. Sometimes dangerously low, causing you to pass out. That is what happened today. Jim, you must eat regular meals."

"So, I don't skip breakfast and lunch, and it won't happen again?"

"Not quite. We will have to do some more testing, and you have to pay attention to everything you eat. Coke Cola is not the answer to this problem. I will arrange a glucose tolerance test and set you up with a dietician as soon as we get those results.

"More tests?" John was disgusted.

"Afraid so, son. There is more."

"More? Can't be more."

"Your blood pressure hasn't responded yet to the medications and is still high. I have a new prescription, and I want to see you every Monday for the next few weeks to see how the medication is controlling."

"More appointments?"

"One more thing . . . "

"No more, Doc. No more! I don't care what you found with your little machines and white coats. No more. No more tests. No more appointments." Jim was getting up and Dr. Belford was alarmed at his agitation.

"Wait. We have to get the IV out before you get up. No more tests or appointments. He had his hands on Jim's shoulders, holding him in the bed. " I have one more prescription—Zocor. Your cholesterol is 281.

Jim just fell back on the pillow. "Whatever."

Grandma had been very quiet and concerned about Jim. She stepped forward and patted his IV'd hand.

"Dear boy, I have my car here to drive you back to my house. I called Marge and she is going to meet us there." Grandma could finally take charge.

Jim folded himself into her little Honda Civic as she handed him a bottle of water and crept out of the parking lot and down Van Dusen Road at thirty miles an hour. It took them eleven minutes and a few seconds to get to Grandma's house.

Chapter 9

Margaret and Sarah

Margaret walked into Sam's at 4:20 and allowed her eyes to get used to the dark room. The jukebox was playing the latest country western ballad. Nora gave her a wave that meant her cheeseburger would be ready soon. "Hi Nora, Heineken today."

"I put your burger on the grill, although you don't often come in two days in a row. Blowin' the diet?"

"Yep. Can't worry about cholesterol; got too much on my mind. It has been a hard day. I just came from the hospital. John fell and broke his hip today."

"No kidding! He was here about noon. So, when did that happen?"

"Must have been right after. He went to Grandma's and fell. He is doing good. Told us to go home."

"That sounds like John. By the way, someone asked about you earlier. The guy you talked to yesterday." Margaret noticed he wasn't at the bar and felt some disappointment, but that didn't last. She would have her burger and beer, head over to Columbia Mall, and spend some time and money.

Nora moved off to tend to her customers and Margaret let herself unwind with the cold beer and music. For the first time since leaving Sarah, she thought about the mystery man in John's life, Harry. She went down the list of everyone she knew named Harry and came up with nothing. So what if John had a male partner; it's his life, not ours. Poor Sarah. She just doesn't deal well with things like this. She nearly had a nervous breakdown over Rock Hudson—threw out her complete VCR collection of his movies. It wasn't that she had a problem with homosexuality, but she had a thing for Rock and felt betrayed. There was a good chance she would have the same problem with John's bent. Sarah would do well to spend some time on a bar stool and maybe do a little boot scooting' boogie with a stranger on the dance floor. Margaret loved her sister very much but felt a failure in bringing her to the mainstream and more meaningful things in life. Margaret felt bad because the only advice she could think to give Sarah to keep her from worrying about John would be: "You already have enough to worry about."

Margaret finished her dinner, waved good-bye to Nora, and decided to drive by Sarah's before heading to the mall—it was on the way if she took Fourth Street. Things were very quiet there, no extra cars, no kids in the yard, so Margaret went in. "Sarah!" The house was eerie quiet.

"Up here, Maggie," came a voice from the upstairs master suite. "I am taking a bath."

Sarah was behind a bank of bubbles at least twelve inches higher than the tub. Candles burned along the vanity, and the aroma of Christmas spice, strawberry, and vanilla filled the air. Sarah popped her head up, and her curly hair was matted to her shiny head. The warm bath and humid air gave her rosy cheeks and the candles made her eyes sparkle.

"Wow, Sarah! You are really into it, aren't you?'

"About an hour. I had to do something to escape and run away. This bathroom was as far as I got, so instead of closing that door and sitting on the toilet, I decided to try the aroma bath you brag about. I even went to my Christmas chest to find these candles."

Margaret spread a towel on the toilet seat and sat down. Sarah seemed relaxed and ready to talk. They didn't have many moments like this, especially in Sarah's house.

"Where is everybody? I don't think I ever saw you home alone before."

"I sent the grandkids home. Haven't answered the phone. I'm sure Vicki (daughter) has called, but I let it go to voice mail. Let her think I'm out shopping or something. Maybe good for her to stay home with her own kids for a change."

"Amen!"

Sarah proceeded to explain that she put the whole bottle of Strawberry Cupcake bubble bath, which belonged to Samantha (aged 4), and a whole bottle of McCormick's Vanilla in the bath. She kept adding hot water to keep the bath warm, so the bubbles went up and up and up. "I like to see the candles through the bubbles; it is like a million little prisms in here. I am surrounded by rainbows."

"Sarah, have you been drinking?"

"No, but I thought about it. Just didn't want to get out of the tub to get it."

"What'cha got? I'll get us some."

"There is a jug of Chardonnay in the refrig. Get plastic glasses."

Sarah returned with the wine, a bag of ice, and two glasses suitable for drinking wine in a bathroom. She poured the drinks and iced the jug in the basin. Sarah reached from her bubble curtain, got her glass, and toasted Margaret.

"Cheers, Sis."

They tipped the glass to each other and continued the visit.

"Where's Tom?"

"Gone."

"Gone where?"

"I'm not sure, but he won't be back before Sunday night. We had a big fight. Tom needed some space." Sarah pulled back a wall of bubbles to see Margaret. "Can you believe? He is sick of our family. He said, sick to death. Thinks he will puke if he hears one of your names. He doesn't want to hear a message from any of the *kooks* on the answer machine; doesn't want to go to the hospital to visit any of my *kooks*; and he especially doesn't want to hear how hard my day is because of the *kooks*. How do you like that? He thinks you are a kook." She lifted one finger off her wine glass to point to her sister. "Tom came this close to calling me a 'kook' too. Sarah tried to demonstrate how close with her thumb and forefinger, but a bubble was in the way.

Margaret softly giggled.

"He did kiss me goodbye and said he would call. He's not *leaving* me."

"No, he wouldn't leave you. He loves you."

"I don't know if I should be angry or hurt or what?"

"I don't think you should be angry or hurt. Why not listen to what he says? Tom is right, you know."

"You think we are all kooks, too?"

"Good word; it fits when we take ourselves too seriously. Tom certainly doesn't hurt my feelings. In fact, I think he makes a lot of sense. He's not talking about us so much as he is talking to you. You worry for everyone, and we all know it. Maybe you should stop worrying about us and Grandma and start worrying about Tom having to get away and you retreating to a bathroom."

"Suppose Grandma does have something terminal. Suppose she is dying?"

"So . . . what can you or any of us do about it? Same thing goes for John. He is going to do fine with the hip replacement, and if he is gay . . . what can worry do for that?"

Sarah was listening, drinking her wine and lifting her glass for a refill. No doubt the wine was expanding Sarah's mind and softening her outlook much as the bubble bath was softening her body.

"If Grandma is saying her good-byes, and signed up for a wine appreciation class, she knows what she is doing. She surely doesn't want us to step in and make her be morbid about it if she doesn't want to be. I never shoulda told you what she said. Damn me."

"I needed to know."

"No, you didn't!" Margaret insisted. "Sis. You go overboard trying to control everything. I know how Tom feels. There are times I hate to hit the play-back button on my answering machine. This family makes me feel like puking sometimes, too."

Margaret tipped the jug to refill her glass and her sister's, too. "Tom should be right here sitting on this toilet watching you take a bath. Why not worry about the fact that your baby sister is here instead . . . and you don't even know where he is." Margaret took a breath and a moment to think. "If I was in that tub and there was a man available, he would be in it with me. If that didn't occur to you, Sarah, you have some real problems."

Margaret envied her sister's marriage and the fact that she had a husband who adored her and at least tried to put up with this crazy family.

Sarah splashed some bubbles on Margaret. When Margaret tried to push Sarah under, her sister dragged her into the tub. The laughing, screaming sisters were a sight, but no one was there to behold them. Margaret was not too happy about getting her shoes wet, but it was worth it to see Sarah having a good time. The two bodies in the already over-full tub caused a tsunami. The water washed over and down the hallway.

"I hope these jeans don't shrink; I think it would strangle me to death. Can you die of strangulation of the crotch?" That did it! The two sisters were kids again with a giggle fit that would not stop and went to hysterics when the wet slippery bodies, well lubricated with chardonnay, tried to untangle and climb the mountainous wall of the tub.

"You go first," they managed to say at the same time, which caused more laughter. Finally, Sarah got out of the tub, followed by Margaret, who struggled to move in her wet, tight jeans. Margaret struggled to stay on her feet, grabbed two towels, and gave one to her naked sister.

"I have to get out of these. Do you have some sweats I can put on?" Margaret began peeling off the jeans.

They were moving toward the bedroom when the water on

the floor caused Sarah to go ass-over-tea-cup in the hallway. Margaret rushed to help and took a flying flip. She looked like the cow that jumped over the moon; landed on the other side of Sarah, whose towel was only covering her feet. The boney elbows did the damage. Sarah took a blow to the nose, and Margaret came up holding her forehead just above the left eye.

"Ouch." Sarah cried. She hurt but not enough to stop laughing.

What a sight. Sarah's bare behind crawling toward the bedroom, and Margaret struggling to get up in jeans that would not let her bend. She crawled on all fours like a short-necked giraffe.

"Sarah, get some clothes on. I have seen about all that I can bear . . . no pun intended." That started the giggles all over again.

"You know, my nose really hurts. It may be broken," Sarah reported when she caught her breath.

"I expect I will have a goose egg on my eyebrow," Margaret complained.

They were both wrong. Sarah's nose was not broken, and Margaret did not get a lump over her eye. They both had black eyes by the time they were dressed and sober. Sarah looked in the mirror and wondered how she could explain Margaret accidentally giving her a black eye without telling too many details.

Margaret could not wait to tell how this happened with her drunken, naked, straight-laced sister—including all the hilarious details

Chapter 10

Harry and Harri

"Where's the shovel? I am here to exhume Harry." Jim and Grandma headed to the garden. "Ahh, the dirty rat." Jim became James Cagney. He would find the hairpiece for John.

Jim had no trouble finding it in a shallow hole, looking like a dead rat, just as Grandma described. A muddy mess, needing a lot of attention before they could take it to John.

Grandma brought a bucket of water and Dawn dishwashing liquid to the porch. Jim dropped Harry in the soapy water, which immediately became a mud puddle. A second pail of clean water had to be brought. Harry came cleaner but still dripped *chocolate milk*.

"Bring your shampoo, Grandma and we will wash it one more time."

And so, they did.

"Now it looks like an old, dead rat that had been to Vidal Sassoon." She proclaimed.

The shampoo made the hair shine, but the cap was torn, and there were more bald spots here than on John's head. "There!" Jim proclaimed after mounting it on the porch banister and using a hair dryer. All this effort did not improve the eight-hundred-dollar hairpiece.

"What's the front? What's the back?" He asked as he slid it on his head and turned and turned. They both began to laugh at Harry and the whole experience of exhumation and attempted resurrection.

"I doubt John is going to want that. I will buy him a new one. Where do you buy things like that?" Grandma became serious.

"I think you need to let him get his own replacement. Toupees are personal things, like underwear. I'll give him the bad news. Want to ride along?"

"It's wine club at the senior center today. I'll call him later and tell him I'll pay for a new one."

♣ ♣ ♣

Jim was surprised; John took the news very well. He seemed not to care about a hairpiece that he had named Harry. For something that was so very important two days ago, he seemed very nonchalant about today.

"Well, that was hardly worth the trouble." Jim remarked as he dropped it in the trash can labeled *Non-hazardous waste* and thought maybe it was the medication that mellowed John's attitude. Slightly perturbed at his brother, Jim left with a parting wave. "See ya."

John's pain was a five on the Rate Your Pain smiley face chart on the wall. Everyone seemed fine with number five; John wanted a number one, and the big smile that went with it. It was day three, and the only thing that totally relieved his pain was the 4 to 12 shift nurse, Harriett. When she came in to check his vitals at about 4:15, she had a big smile for him, and he had one for her.

"Hi, beautiful!"

"I guess you say that to all the nurses."

"Only the beautiful ones."

If she was late, say 4:16 or 4:17, his pain level went to six, and he worried that she might not be his nurse this evening. He did not know that she was making sure her charges included the man in Room 2C44. He would have rested easier if he had.

There was something special and different about Harriett that John could not put his finger on. He just liked to look at her. She was probably 45 and so easy on the eyes. About 5' 6" and her figure was hourglass, her smile genuine. He liked her tan complexion, salt and pepper short curly hair, and her smile. Her brown eyes were bright, and she had beautiful laugh lines along her face. He quickly noted she had a sense of humor. John was so taken with her that he was embarrassed when she did her nursely duties, like lifting his gown to check his incision, as if they were maybe old and dear friends. He did have the feeling that he had known her a long time but in truth, he had never seen her before.

Harriett liked John, too. At first, it was his voice, soft and gentlemanly. As she paid more attention to him, she enjoyed his charm and mature good looks. She found him physically attractive, and it was interfering with her job here in Room 2C44, especially when she lifted his gown to check his incision. Harriett had been a nurse for 22 years, and she had never had this happen before. She often got attached to little old men and sweet old women. Never had personal emotion nagged at her in her work. This was certainly different.

John did not want to fall in love again, but it happened. Love did not work for him. Another wife? No, no more. But John loved women, and this beauty had his full attention. For the first time he realized that the women he had been dating were too young. That was the difference that John could not put his finger on. Harriett was the right age for him. He had not had an age-appropriate woman since he married wife number one, his high school sweetheart.

By four in the afternoon, he had convinced himself that this was foolish, and he didn't care if she came in or not. Any nurse would do. By 4:15, his attitude changed; she was the only person he wanted to come into the room.

John began by asking questions while she was tending to him.

"You love your job?"

"Yes, I've always been a nurse. Even as a little girl, I planned to be one. Can't remember when I wasn't."

"How come you work the late shift?"

"I like it so I can do other things during the day."

She didn't say family, he thought.

"Like what?"

"Oh, I sorta have another job; an avocation. I love to sew. I make drapes and pillows. It is a good business, but I would never stop nursing."

"You are a good nurse."

"Thank you. Did you put your menu in for dinner? It will be coming soon."

She was gone, but she would be back. By day five, John knew she was divorced and that her grown son was away at college.

He knew she liked Italian food, line dancing, and movies. They were both Star Wars buffs, and when she came in the room, he was ready with a trivia question for her. She was usually right on with the answer.

"Solo's spaceship. "

"Too easy - the Millennium Falcon."

John and Harriett were becoming good friends, and she was looking forward to seeing him each day, too. His hip was getting better, stronger, and more reliable. He forgot about Harry, the hairpiece. John focused on Harri (Harriett), the nurse.

The doctors were beginning to talk about transferring John to rehab to complete his recovery, and that meant Harriett would not be his nurse. He would not see her every day. His pain level went back up to six.

"Do you ever work up in rehab?"

"No, I am always on the ortho wing." On his last day on her floor, Harriett did not come in to tell John good night before she left at 11:00. By 11:15, he was very upset. After all, what else does a hospitalized man have to look forward to? At 11:30 he was thoroughly upset, feeling as he did when one of his wives (not sure which one) left him. *This is ridiculous!* he told himself as he grabbed his pillow to settle his head and rolled over to go to sleep. At 11:55, something startled him. Harriett was sitting on his bed, looking back at him.

"John, I am sorry I left without saying good night. I felt silly so I ignored my crush on you and went home . . . but I had to come back. I need to say good night and tell you I'll miss you when you leave here." She took a breath.

It took him only a minute to wake up and understand what she was saying.

"I'll miss you, too."

"I care about you. Patients leave here, and I never expect to see them again. Never really cared, but you will be moved tomorrow; I want to be sure I see you again."

"You are going to see me." He saw that she had closed the door when she came in. "We need to get to know each other better." John threw the blanket back. Harriett crawled in beside him. It is a small bed, but the two of them fit very nicely. If it were a king-size bed, they would still be using only this combined space. His geometric print hospital gown and her colorful smock and cotton work clothes blended. They looked like the colors-load for the washing machine. His hip would not allow intercourse, but they were mature adults. They were only together to *get to know each other better.* And they did. They started talking as if they had to catch up on a lifetime.

"I was born in Mississippi and came here as a bride. My ex was from Rockville. My son is the only relative I have here. All the rest are living on the delta mud."

"This is my hometown. The Cottons lived here for generations. I have my daughter, seven brothers and sisters, and their kids. And my grandmother. Just wait until you meet this crazy bunch. Even in the Louisiana Delta, you haven't seen cotton like my family."

He found her appendicitis scar and arthritis in her fingers and knees. She found his slightly rounded belly and vasectomy scar. They laughed about being here in this bed and cried about the hard knocks life had dealt them. Most of all, they held on and felt like teenagers who knew what they wanted but knew they could not have it yet.

Along about 2 a.m. Sandy, the night nurse came in for vitals, pushing her high-tech-everything-machine. As was her practice, she threw open the door to allow enough light from the hall to do her job. She was one of those rare nurses that didn't put the spotlights on sleeping patients in the middle of the night. She quietly rolled the machine to the bed and uncovered the arm, which twisted around another arm. Lifting the covers a bit more, she saw a third arm. To say this stopped her in her tracks is to put it mildly. In fact, for just an instant she was befuddled. The scene on the bed startled her, and she put her hand to her mouth to stifle her own voice. *"There must be another arm in there somewhere . . . and legs."* She thought. The limbs she could see were wound together like Jack's beanstalk.

For the first time, she assessed the mound in the bed. It did not compute with the slim patient she expected. "Harriett," she whispered when she saw the woman's face. The night nurse backed out of the room, closed the door, and repeated the figures for blood pressure and temperature that Harriett had recorded hours earlier.

In the early hours, the couple unwound, and Harriett slipped away. Sandy had stationed herself to see any movement from the room. She saw Harriett take the back stairs and make her exit. Nurses have seen everything and little scenes like this are what keep the job interesting. Amid bare behinds and bedpans, a little soap opera is a welcome diversion. Sandy was good at telling the story, putting the emphasis on just the right words: twisted, arms, legs, tangled bodies. The other night nurses would make a point to check room 2C44 as soon as possible and even take a second look at John Cotton. Maybe they had missed something.

"Did you see who it was?" the morning nurses asked.

"Yeah. I saw her but didn't know her," Sandy lied. They all went down to see. John was snoring alone.

"Maybe this was one of Sandy's jokes."

"He is right cute in an old sort of way."

"Not my type."

"You know as well as I; you don't know what's under the covers without looking." She lifted the sheet to see if she could see anything significant.

"Well, I've seen a lot of them; it would have to be something to impress me."

"Just another man. Must'a got lucky."

John awoke in the morning wondering if he had dreamt it. He also awoke with a wonderful feeling of anticipation. During the morning, he had excellent nurse services—more than usual and a different nurse every time. They were constantly checking his incision. John was getting a little tired of this lifting of the sheet and gown.

"I think I have had every nurse in this hospital come in here this morning. It must be part of the preparation to move me." He told Sarah when she called to see if he wanted her to bring some reading material.

Later that afternoon, Harriett came in a little early to see him before he was moved off her floor. She stepped into John's room to greet him as he was saying on the phone ... "So, Harry is dead, mutilated! Good riddance. ... It didn't matter how deep you dug the grave. ... If the police hadn't come, we could have gotten this all taken care of days ago. Don't worry who will pay for it; it won't be you. If anyone, it will be me." Harriett ran from the room, devastated and sure she did not know John very well at all.

Dead. Buried. Mutilated. Police. Harriett leaned against the wall to collect herself. She was so upset it was evident to another nurse in the corridor. "Are you OK, Harri," she inquired, taking her hand and leading her to the nurse's station.

"I'll be fine; I just need a moment. Felt a little lightheaded." Harriett could not collect her thoughts and concentration. She asked the head nurse to get coverage so she could go home.

Harriett left John's room without hearing him break into laughter with Grandma. "What a story, Grandma. To tell you the truth, I have fallen in love with a nurse here and she has never seen me *with* a toupee. I think I have found the right one this time and if she is, I'll never wear one again. *Harry Toupee* and I are through." John leaned back in his happiness and prepared for his move to rehab, knowing that Harriett would have information on his new room number on the fourth-floor Rehabilitation Unit.

John hoped she would get here before he was moved, but he could wait until 11:15 if he had too. He watched for her beautiful form in the hallways as he was transported by wheelchair to the fourth floor, but she was not to be seen. The time came and went. Her shift was over. She did not come. Hours went by; he did not close his eyes. Where could she be? Had she had an accident, an emergency? John's bliss was gone, and he was frantic. He was crippled, helpless, and unhappy and had no way to reach her.

Last night did happen. Harriett had come to his bed. He was sure it was not a dream. The conversations and the touching happened, he was sure . . . or was he? Thoughts that it might have been a dream made everything worse . . . his life, his hip, and his future. He ran his hand over his baldhead and wished he had the phone number to order another *Harry*.

The next afternoon when Grandma came to rehab to visit John, he was a depressed man. Nothing cheered him up, not even her embroidered blouse with the bowling ball and pins on the back and a big peacock across the front. It was a bright blue, multicolored design with sequins. She had a feathered comb pushed into her hair. She wanted John to see her dressed for the bowling banquet this evening since he was the only one of her grandchildren who understood her natural flair for dress. Grandma's mood was light. Beads that sparkle always made her feel like part of the sunny day, especially when she saw them reflecting on the walls. Her grandson did not notice her beautiful shirt.

"How do you like my bowling shirt? See the sequins I put on myself. We are the 'Proud Peacocks' and won first place. I'm on my way to the banquet at the American Legion. I wish you could go with me."

"Sorry, Grandma. Not this year." There was no lift in his voice and no compliments on her dress either.

"Dear, dear John. What is wrong? Isn't rehab going well? You're down in the mouth."

"It's going good. I will be out of here in two more days."

"Well, what is the matter? Why the sour puss? Are you still upset about your hairpiece? I told you! You look better without it."

"Nah, Grandma, I'm not worried about ole Harry. I can always get another. It's like this. I met this special nurse, Harriett, and we became friends, very good friends and she was to come up to rehab to see me. I am afraid something happened to her. She was on the second floor and worked the 4 to 11 shift. I called there, and they just take my messages. I can't seem to find her."

"What's her name?"

"Harriett Stowe." John uttered dejectedly.

Grandma kissed her grandson goodbye, patted him on his bald head and headed for the elevator. She was off to the second floor to find his nurse. That is what Grandmas are for.

"Harriett Stowe, you are wanted at the nurse's station." She was paged for the little ole lady. As Harriett came down the corridor, Grandma could see why John was smitten. She was lovely and just the right age; that pleased Grandma.

"Hello, I am Harriett Stowe. Do you have a relative on this floor?"

"No, my grandson is on the fourth floor."

"You had me paged?"

"Yes, I wanted to have a look at you since he wants to see you so badly. My name is Lucille Cotton." Harriett could not help noticing every sparkle about the little woman and she liked her immediately.

"You are John's grandmother? He sent you here?"

"Yes. No, he didn't send me, but he told me you were not returning his messages. I wanted to see who could spin his head since he has been dead set against women for a while now."

"Mrs. Cotton, I am really very busy. We have nothing to talk about."

"A minute, please." Grandma looked her most vulnerable and coaxing. "Please."

They moved to a lounge and sat.

"He said something about Harry." Harriett opened but didn't know how to discuss the troubling conversation she had overheard.

It seemed stupid to be asked about the toupee but if that is what's bothering her, Grandma would oblige.

"Well ... I don't have much time either, Miss Stowe. I have a bowling banquet. I will tell you quickly. John left Harry at my house. I didn't mean any harm. I thought the best thing was to dig a spot in the garden after a few blows with the floor lamp. Mark, John's brother, tried to dig Harry up but the police came. After all that, John just said forget it. I would not have to pay. Personally, I think John looks better now that Harry is gone."

Those words did not help Harriett. Her head was spinning. *I've got to get out of here.* She stood to leave. Grandma took her arm. "This is none of my business."

"I just wish you would go up and see John. He really wants to see you and I think his recovery will be delayed if you don't. Go for medical reasons, if not any other."

Harriett was confounded and confused. She was sure that she did not want to be involved with John or his Grandmother. How could her heart be so broken over a man she hardly knew? "I must go now. I have patients." She pulled her arm away and moved toward the door.

Grandma could not be deterred. She reached for Harriett's arm again. "Don't you think John is handsome enough and doesn't need to wear a hairpiece? So silly to name a toupee Harry? You tell me. It was all my fault. I thought it was a rat, and I buried it."

Grandma, the little tornado, made Harriett's head spin in another direction as if she had just landed in Oz. She didn't know whether to laugh or cry. Harriett folded back into the chair.

"Harry is a toupee—a hairpiece! You killed and buried a hairpiece!" Harriett hugged Grandma and ran for the door. "This was all about a toupee?"

Grandma nodded. "Yes. The police had a hard time understanding, too. But we got it sorted out."

"God, you are spectacular!" Harriett took hold of the sequined-plumed lady, lifted her off the floor with a bear hug, and went for the door.

"Are you going to John?" Grandma shouted across the room.

"Yes!" Echoed back from the hallway.

♪ ♪ ♪

John had somehow lost Harriett. It was a serious reflective time for the depressed man. A harsh reality—either she wasn't the woman she presented, or he wasn't the man to hold her. John was not meant to find love again, so he prepared his mind to return to a lifestyle with no basis. He turned his thoughts and faced the blank hospital wall with a sigh.

Harriett came right to him, pulled him from the wall, and gave him a kiss. She decided not to tell him about over-hearing his phone conversation, the confusion over Harry, or his Grandmother's visit.

John was so glad to see her that he didn't ask any questions about the past 24 hours.

"I was beginning to believe I was dreaming the last time I saw you."

"It was real. Forget the day between that time and now. Come closer." She kissed him between each statement.

John didn't care about her words, he welcomed and savored each kiss.

"When are you getting released? You will need someone to help when you go home." Harriett kissed him again. "See, John, it is a good thing that I work 4 to 11. You can sleep when I'm at work." Kiss.

John left the hospital with a new hip joint, a bald head, his own private duty nurse and.... Love.

Chapter 11

Grandma and Doc

Grandma was in a hurry. She had told a little white lie to John and Harriett. Her bowling banquet was not until 6 o'clock. She did not want them to know she was going to see Doc Belford before going to the Legion Hall.

Dr. Belford's waiting room was empty. The nurses did not set appointments after 3:30 on a Friday afternoon. Lucille Cotton was the exception. Doctor Belford set this appointment himself. Besides, they liked to have her come in and brighten the office just before the weekend started. Today was no different—Lucille came dressed as a peacock. Her cheeks were rosy and eyes smiling. "Doctor Belford will be right with you, Mrs. Cotton," Judy advised.

He was waiting for her in the examination room, which never happens with his other patients. Even knowing what he did about her diagnosis, this would not be a somber meeting.

"Hello, Lucille." he said, putting his arm around her shoulder and leading her to the chair.

"Hi, Doc. Why do you want to talk to me again? I thought we had it all worked out. I suspect you have a crush on me and that's why you called me back in."

"I do have a crush on you and always have, but you chose Irving back in school, and I didn't stand a chance."

"Maybe you should have told me sooner we could have set this little town on its ear." she laughed.

"Now it is hard to remember just what I wanted to do with you." The doctor joked as he pulled up a chair and sat across from his favorite patient. "I am going to retire this summer. We are the same age, and I have worked way past my prime. Only a few old-timers make appointments to see me. Dr. Franklin has really taken over. I am only here a few hours a week."

"I hope you have something to look forward to. What are you going to do with yourself?" Lucille asked.

"Hold on to your feathers, ole girl," he smiled. "I want to take that trip with you." For the first time in longer than she could remember, Grandma was at a loss for words.

She reached for her feathers and pushed the comb snugly into her red curls. Dealing with her grandchildren, she was used to fielding the unexpected, but this came at her from left field. She swallowed, took a deep breath, and began her infectious laugh, which he joined. She stopped laughing and looked up at him.

"You want to go to Spain, too?"

"Yep."

"You're serious, aren't you?"

"Absolutely."

"You want to go to Spain," she repeated.

"Honestly, I never thought of Spain until you came in talking about it. I decided, why not Spain? I would never plan to go off alone like you are. But because of you—I want to go to Spain. I want to make that trip with you."

"You have decided I need a doctor on my trip."

"No. You don't need a doctor; you need a friend to travel with. I want to go with you. It is as simple as that. I told you traveling would not make a bit of difference to the outcome of your illness. You will feel good until it catches up with you. We are the same, Lucille, and I appreciate your outlook and desire to use your time wisely. If you don't want to spend the time you have left fighting with medicines that make you sicker, if you want to take a trip you've always dreamed of, it is your choice. Who knows, I may die before you."

"Are you sick?"

"No," he lied. In truth, he had a different diagnosis but the same prognosis as she. Lucille's decision to live what time she had on her terms made wonderful sense to him. There was no one he would rather spend his own precious time with. Without her courage, he would die in this tiny room, wearing his white coat and a necklace stethoscope.

"I had to keep the truth from Jim when he was here the other day, but that is your choice, too. I had to follow your wishes."

"Thanks, Doc. I want to give the kids the same time I have chosen for myself. I want them to be as happy as I intend to be during the next year - if I have a year."

"Lucille, you are amazing. Can I go? Please?" He sounded like a little boy asking for an extra piece of candy.

She didn't move; did not make a sound. He was sure his appeal would be denied. Lucille was thinking carefully about his proposal. She put her finger to her mouth to keep him from talking while she thought. He folded his arms across his chest and leaned back into his chair to wait for her words.

"Isn't it strange Doc? When we get to an age where we are sure what we want to do, we are forced back into that stage when we worry about what others think. Years ago, I learned not to worry what anyone thought and here I am worrying about what my family will think if we go off on a trip together."

"I don't know much about that, not having any children of my own." He rarely thought after all these years about the torch he carried for Lucille Cunningham. It crossed his mind today, sitting across from her. He never had time for a wife and family after he dedicated his life to caring for every other family in Laurel.

"The grandchildren have opinions. Thankfully, the five great-grandchildren don't yet. I want them to let me go, figuratively, but more than that, I want them to let go for themselves."

"Do they object to your trip?"

"They don't even know about Spain. Haven't had time to object. Maybe with you going, they will object less."

"Jim knows you want to take a trip. It came out when he was here. Maybe they will object more if I go. Consider that."

"More or less, what's the difference? Let's do it! Why not? I had planned to join a tour group but even in a group of Senior citizens, it would be better if I have someone special with me. You sure fill that bill."

"Honestly, I can't recall when I have been so happy making a plan. I'm truly excited and sure we will have a wonderful time."

"Come for dinner Sunday after church. I will show you the travel brochures and tour company. You cannot imagine how those kids will fall all over each other trying to keep me home if they have time to think about it or suspect I have cancer. Don't tell Judy the purpose of this appointment," she joked. "There are no secrets in this town, and I wouldn't want the kids to know before I tell them."

"Now, I do have something to look forward to in retirement. It will be great."

"We have to talk details, sleeping arrangements and things like that."

"Well, at our age, it will be a pleasure talking about it." The old friends shared a bear hug. He escorted her out the waiting room door.

"See you Sunday. Come hungry". There was no embarrassment or self-consciousness between them, even as the girls at the desk giggled. She went to the bowling banquet with an extra lilt in her step, bright color in her cheeks, a broad smile on her face, and a wonderful secret. To her friends assembled, she looked the same as always.

Doc was whistling when he hung up his stethoscope and white coat. He stopped by the mirror to smile at himself before going home.

🐟 🐟 🐟

"I had an appointment with Doc Belford," Lucille announced when Snow White met her at the door. "Before the banquet. It's been quite a day, Snow."

"Could I eat first? It's past time." Snow White circled her dish.

"Doc Belford is going to Spain with me."

"Really?" Snow acted only half interested as she ate.

"I wanted to talk to you about it. Get your opinion."

Snow walked to Lucille, inviting her to lift her onto her lap. "I don't have an opinion and won't until you think it over and decide what you think about it."

"You're right. I have ta' think about it. Tomorrow." She scooted the cat off the table. "Ready for bed?"

Snow White skittered up the stairs and greeted Lucille in the bedroom.

"Doc Belford...hmm," was the only thing Snow White said before the light went out.

Chapter 12

Mark and Grandma

Tuesday at noon Fredrico arrived to have lunch before they went to the stables. Lucille loved this time as Fredrico enjoyed whatever she prepared, and she didn't have to eat alone. Mealtime was the worst to be alone. She missed Irving when she sat the food on the table with only one placemat. Fredrico seldom declined the invitation. During lunch, she taught him English. He could name many foods, and the utensils used to eat them, plus some important communication phrases. Before leaving for the stable, she always wrote his check for today's lesson, which included the tip. She pushed the travel brochures aside and made room for their plates with egg salad sandwiches and chips. As they were about to take a bite, Mark came in.

"Grandma," he called.

"In here, dear. Want some lunch?"

Mark, with all those years as an analyst for the DOD, started gathering intelligence as soon as he entered the room. His mind was reading, sorting, and decoding what he was seeing in

Grandma's dining room. He shook his head to the invitation to eat. No.

Grandma. Young stranger. Travel brochure. Airline tickets. Checkbook. Trouble with a capital "T". The facts filled his brain.

"I would like you to meet Fredrico, my riding teacher. Fredrico: My grandson, Mark."

Mark extended his hand and said, "You from around here?"

"Sorry, Mark, he doesn't speak English. He's from Madrid; that's in Spain."

"I know it is in Spain."

"Have a sandwich. It's egg salad." Mark shook his head again; he was still gathering intelligence. *The stranger seemed to be right at home.*

"Would you like to go to see me ride? We were about to leave." Mark shook his head. His mind was so busy he could not even carry the conversation with Grandma as if suddenly he didn't speak English either.

"I hate to go off when you have just gotten here. Will you be here when we get back?" Lucille quizzed Mark.

Mark had second thoughts. "I'll come, too."

As he drove, Mark did not remember traveling out of town, down Route 216 to Gorman Road, but suddenly, he was at the riding stable. He did not recall traveling past Margaret's house or down Leisure Road. His mind was too busy trying to decide what to do about Grandma going to a riding stable with a foreign stranger. *Maybe Sarah was right.* Another thought squeezed into his brain.

Mark surveyed the area and climbed on the fence around the corral to have a good view of Grandma and Fredrico. It was surprising to see how well she did on the horse. Fredrico had the lead in his hands, and the horse never broke his gait as he went around the paddock.

Grandma seemed so happy and proud in the saddle. She waved to Mark. It was special to have him watching her from the top railing. She smiled broadly each time she passed.

"Watch Mark! He's going to let me go by myself." Grandma shouted. Mark was riveted to his perch on the fence. He was not going anywhere. He wanted to see Grandma take her turn around the circle alone. Climbing on that horse took a lot of courage, and he was gaining admiration for her by the minute. At the far end of the corral, Fredrico was mounting a horse, and the two of them came around with the horses matching their gait. Her coach stayed very close and never took his eyes off Grandma and her horse. It was obvious she was enjoying herself.

"Mark, why don't you come and ride with us?" It would be awkward to explain that he was afraid of horses and would never attempt to ride one.

If Mark had gone into the bunkhouse at the far end of the corral, he would have seen the notice about the program for seniors here at the Gorman Road Stables. Maybe he would have been more at ease if he knew that Fredrico was listed as one of the coaches in the program. Cost - $20.00 per hour. Endorsed by the Senior Olympics Committee and The United Way.

"Can I take you home?" He asked as Grandma walked toward him after completing her lesson for the day.

"Sure. That would be fine. Fredrico has to cool off the horses and put the gear away. I'll be ready as soon as I tell him."

The ride home was quiet because Grandma fell asleep as soon as the car started moving. That gave Mark time to think about the things he wanted to talk to her about. He was proud of Grandma and had a sincere interest in what she planned to do next. His attitude changed while he sat on that railing and watched her do something he could never do.

"Come in and have some dinner with me?"

"Let's go to the diner and have a burger. I'll call Pam while you change; it is only 5:20." Grandma was delighted with this plan and glad to have time to change into a nice outfit for her date with her grandson.

Mark put his stiff white collar in his pocket.

Grandma chose jeans and her Beach Boys tee-shirt from the concert at Merryweather Post Pavilion last fall. It had Brian, Dennis, Carl, Mike and Al, on the front and Surfin' USA on the back in great beach colors. The tee shirt came down to her knees. Her earrings were hot pink surfboards. Just before going out the door, she parked her Elton John sunglasses on her head as if they were her hat. "I'm ready!"

Her appearance lifted his spirits and the weighty things that had brought him here seemed way off. Mark gave her a big hug and said, "You're ready; I'm ready. Let's go."

"How about a Spartan Burger, Grandma? " He ordered the burgers, named after the Laurel High sports teams, and chocolate shakes. When the food was brought, Grandma dumped a pile of catsup on the French fries. Mark put a quarter in the jukebox to play "California Girls" and wished more than anything that he had on jeans and a leather jacket. Their mood was special. It had been a long time since these two had shared any part of their lives.

"I'm glad I went to the stables with you and saw how much you enjoy horseback riding," Mark opened the conversation.

"I'm glad, too. I love it, and I won't tell you how long it has taken me to get over being afraid. I was sure I couldn't do it. The funny thing was, since Fredrico couldn't understand English, I had no way to tell him I was afraid. He just moved me ahead into the saddle. Now, I am not afraid. I feel brave and I think I can do other things since I have mastered the fear of horses."

"Like being in the Senior Olympics?" Mark asked.

"Senior Olympics?"

"Are you preparing for the Senior Olympics?"

"Heavens, no. I've no interest in that. Where did you get that idea?" She asked.

"Sarah."

"Oh dear. I should have known. I'll have to tell her, or she'll worry about that. Sarah's always looking for something to worry about. I don't worry much, but I've been worried about you, Mark, since you were arrested at my house, and they thought you were kidnapping me. Do you have a criminal record now? That wouldn't be good for a clergy."

"I was only booked, not charged, and Pete got the whole thing straightened out."

"This family needs a lawyer; glad we got Pete." Grandma stopped worrying about Mark's criminal record. As a rule, she did not worry about anything for more than two days. Most times it takes a whole day or more to figure out what these kids are about. A big bite of the burger, a long draw of sweet chocolate milkshake, and she was ready to change the subject.

"I am proud of you, grandson. I never thought we would have an ordination in the family. I didn't know what you had to do to be a deacon in the Catholic Church, so I read up on it. You started seminary and didn't tell anyone."

"It was a *suppose-I-don't-succeed* attitude. I wanted to be absolutely sure before I told anyone except Pam. The decision was a long time coming. Now that it is accomplished, I have some misgivings that I can live up to it."

"I have wondered if your career at NSA influenced you to go into the ministry. It just seems so far from being a spy." Mark had to laugh at her easy use of the word *spy*. He thought of himself as an analyst and embraced his silence whenever anyone referred to him differently. Tonight, he would make an exception and answer his grandmother.

"Well Grandma . . . I guess it is like this. I love my country and am proud of my service through my work, which is very important to the security and freedom we enjoy. I have always felt God and Country went together. Now my emphasis is on the God part." She took his hand as he continued. "I'm having my doubts; maybe this new avocation is a mistake. I don't seem to be making a difference, and my own family doesn't take me seriously. Sorry, Grandma, didn't want to spoil your dinner with my whining."

"You know what they say about a prophet and his own hometown." She proceeded with a mouth full of fries dripping catsup. "Jesus couldn't preach in Nazareth, and I suspect He would have had a hard time in Laurel with the Cottons. You are a good man, Mark. You aren't God, and he doesn't expect for you to look for perfection in yourself." A dollop of catsup traveled from her burger to her T-shirt and blended in with the beach boys and the bright colors. "You have only been ordained a few months, give yourself self some time to get comfortable."

"Frankly, I'm thinking about hanging this collar up."

She took another draw on her shake and took a moment to

enjoy the sweet, cool chocolate.

"That is what I would suggest—park that collar—permanently." He instinctively moved his hand to his throat to feel it gone and then to the pocket where it was ready to unfold to perfect stiffness. He was instantly disappointed as Grandma's remark went straight to his heart.

"You think I should give up ministry?"

"Not ministry . . . the collar. The collar is the problem. Give up advertising, which is what that collar is. Live the life. Don't walk around with that white stripe around your throat, expecting it to make you different; different to others and to yourself. Ditch the collar and get comfortable in your new skin." She turned her attention to the last few bites of her dinner and gave Mark time to think about what she said.

"You think I should stay in the ministry and continue to be the deacon at St Mary's?"

"Try it a few months without the collar. That is what I'm saying." The straw in her glass sounded like a gorilla clearing its throat. She did it one more time for the last delicious drop. "You aren't expected to be perfect, but if everything you do is according to the Golden Rule, you will be an outstanding disciple. I have something for you."

Grandma began rummaging in her purse and came up with a tiny box and handed it to him. Inside was a small gold cross with a stickpin back.

"This is my cross, given to me when I was confirmed. I had the stickpin put on it. Why not wear that on your shirt." She reached across and put the shiny little cross on his shirt pocket above his heart and patted him lovingly.

Mark watched her as she devoured her meal and took

delight in every French fry and the last drop of catsup. He was feeling a great love for her, plus recalling the admiration that he had had for her since childhood.

When they got back to A Street, Mark walked her in and turned the light on before heading home. He was again faced with the piles of travel brochures on the table.

"Sarah thinks I should do some traveling. I have been thinking about it." Grandma addressed his interest in her messy table.

"Really?" It surprised him that Sarah would endorse anything so adventuresome.

"She gave me these books to read, and they are inviting. Just makes you want to go." She was showing the collection of books in the magazine rack and spread on the table. "Of course, you have been everywhere. Have you ever been to Spain?" Mark had been to Spain, to Australia, Italy, Japan and most European countries courtesy of the Department of Defense. But he did not want to tell Grandma how exciting and wonderful those places are and be responsible for her decision to go. Leave that up to Sarah. Maybe Sarah is planning on going with her. He didn't know.

"I've been reading these books, and I wish I could go see them all.

"You have already bought a ticket?" He asked as he picked up the envelope from American Airlines.

"It is one of those American Airline's senior fares that can be used anytime and be traded up. Buy it for $200.00 and hold on to it until you are ready to go. And it promises priority seating. Give them six weeks' notice and a credit card number; they will calculate the fare and add it to your credit card and ticket.

I won the jackpot at the fire hall bingo Wednesday night, so I bought the ticket to keep me motivated." She stopped short of mentioning Doc. She wanted Mark to say *good for you* or some encouraging word, but he wasn't positive Sarah was part of this.

Grandma expected Mark to ask who was going with her, but he didn't. It never occurred to her that he thought Sarah was going too.

Mark was funny that way. He gathered intelligence but did not ask questions. His profession of gathering information did not include asking questions. He was trained to listen and analyze. He was also trained in the *need-to-know theory*. Unless he could see his role in the action, he would rather not know about it. This was Sarah's action. He had enough of Grandma's equestrian life stored on his brain chips, and he was past ready to exit from 206 A Street. "Are you going soon?" It was the only question he allowed himself.

"I'm still in the planning stage." That satisfied Mark. He made his exit with a kiss on the precious, soft cheek as he fingered the tiny cross pinned on the pocket over his heart.

Chapter 13

Snow White

It had been a good day. Lucille kicked off her sneakers and pulled off her tee shirt to treat the catsup stain. Snow White sauntered into the laundry room and walked over Lucille's feet, caressing her ankles with her long tail.

"You could at least say hello." Lucille chastised.

"You have your way; I have mine," the arrogant cat responded.

"Come upstairs with me and I'll tell you about the cheeseburger and shake Mark and I had at the diner."

Upstairs, sitting in her cozy pajamas, watching Wheel of Fortune with Snow White on her lap, Lucille finished the day.

"I had such a good day riding and then to the diner. The best was time with Mark."

"I know, I know," Snow White responded, hoping for better conversation.

"He is really a fine person, a gentle soul, one of the shining stars."

"You think they are all stars." Snow stretched and arched her back. "Me, not so much."

"I can't have favorites."

But you do." Snow White looked up at her. "You surely do."

"I have to decide your next home." Lucille changed the subject. "Should I consider Mark. He's friendly to you, and I've noticed you don't leave the room when he's here.

"Mark has a dog."

"Oh, you're right. How'd you know?"

"Believe me, if you are down there walking around shoes—you know who has a dog. Mark has a dog, Sarah has a dog, Pete has a dog. Not sure about Matt. Did his dog die?"

"Yes. but he's getting a puppy soon. You're so smart," she accused.

"That narrows the field." Snow White *spifft* as she headed to her bed.

"Can we talk about it?" Lucille appealed. Snow White continued strutting as if entering a five-star hotel. She circled her bed and tossed her long white tail across her back as if they were Lady Aster's pearls.

"Sometimes you are impossible. Pig-headed and too damn independent," Lucille accused her cat without a smile.

She knew why Snow White moved from her lap and left her with her agonies. Snow did not want to think about a home without Lucille. That cat didn't want to think about it anymore than Lucille did. In the quiet of the evening, especially after a happy time with Mark, troublesome thinking clouded Lucille's mind. Troublesome on every level. Facing Snow White's future brought a full glaring scenario. She had made compensations, rationalization, and concessions for choices for herself, but voicing them with Snow forced her to look at them again and face her doubts and fears. It sapped her confidence. She wished, at this moment, that she was curled up in a luxury bed with a fur boa, too.

Lucille could not sleep. She went back to the kitchen. No point in asking Snow to go with her. She had to go alone. As she drank the warm tea, she became more troubled and agitated about her beloved cat. Snow White's future was important. Her comfort. Her day-to-day existence. Her possible demise—after all she was eleven years old. How would she be in a strange environment. *How would she get along without me?*—the most troubling thought.

Lucille wasn't far into her cup of tea when Snow White drifted into the kitchen.

"You are thinking so loud, I couldn't sleep." Snow proclaimed as she climbed onto the closest chair, walked gingerly over the table clutter, and sat facing Lucille. "You aren't making a mistake. Do I have to tell you again?" Lucille embraced Snow's head and gently pulled her onto her lap. "Nothing makes more sense than following your instincts. You don't have to cement here because those kids need to come in and out of this house like it is true north on the compass. It's a trip to Spain, for heaven's sake. People do it every day. A chance to see the world—at least some of it. Only today is promised if you are in Spain or at the bowling alley. No traveler knows if they will be alive from a trip to Spain or a trip to the grocery store."

"Snow, I wish I had more time."

"If wishes were fishes, we'd have a basket full." Snow recited the old adage.

"I most likely will not come back."

"You have made a choice. Period."

"Hey, Ole Girl, I think Irving is getting a big kick out of this and cheering you on."

"Do you really believe that?"

"I have powers. I know," Snow purred. "I know," she repeated, leaving no doubt. "I know other things, too."

"I'm not so sure you know anything. I hate it when you act so superior. Love you . . . I do, but you're just a cat."

Snow White proudly, like a ballerina, pounced to the floor. "To bed, Lucille. Fiddle-lee-dee. Tomorrow is another day."

Chapter 14

Fredrico

Fredrico really did not mean to mislead Lucille Cotton. He wanted to do his job with the least amount of trouble. His job was to get his pupil on the horse. What better way to assure that than professing ignorance of the English language. No arguments.

A few weeks ago, he drove through the Howard County hills that reminded him of his home in Spain. Coming upon the riding stable and ring on Gorman Road was a surprise. Frederico drove in to watch the riders. It was rare that he could get away from his responsibilities at the track. Finding Gorman Road Riding Center was rejuvenating for him.

"You from the Racetrack? Come on in. I'll tell you about the program." A voice surprised him at the car window. "We really need instructors. Did you see our ad at the track?" The man either didn't see Fredrico shake his head, or he ignored it. "Come on in." The man repeated the invitation and opened the car door.

Fredrico went it, and before he knew it, he had committed to one day a week with a senior citizen at the Gorman Road Riding Center and School. He felt surprisingly good about it. This could be just what he needed to overcome homesickness and boredom. He missed Spain, He missed his family. And he couldn't stay at the track 24/7.

Lucille came into the Gorman Riding Center with several other seniors from the Laurel Senior Center to sign up for the senior equestrian program. They would participate in a six-week class especially designed by the Senior Olympics Committee.

This was Fredrico's third session with the seniors. He was assigned to Lucille as her one-on-one teacher. He knew pretending not to understand English was the only way to approach his students. He had learned in the first session that seniors talk your ear off about their past. And they tell the same story over and over. His new student was told *non compendia.* Lucille Cotton got right to the lesson. When she hesitated to get on the horse, he pretended not to know she was frightened. It worked. Not one of his students quit without riding a horse.

Fredrico was the most successful instructor, and he loved doing it. He gave the money he earned to animal rescue, earmarked for horses.

Lucile Cotton was the only woman in this class and the oldest, too. But, the liveliest, no doubt. She came dressed in jeans with a pressed crease down each leg and a white shirt with the collar up in the back. The scarf around her neck was a red bandana. Her earrings were tiny tri-colored foxhounds dangling onto the white collar.

"I'm Lucille Cotton, you can call me Lucy."

Fredrico never called her Lucy. He decided to call her

Lucinda.

"Lucinda," he greeted, as he put his finger into his chest and said, "Fredrico. No speaka de Englash."

Lucille nodded and, without missing a beat, pulled up her pant leg to show him her new riding boots.

Fredrico flashed his most charming smile. The two of them began to love each other right then. It was one of those special bonds that is difficult to explain outside of romance, age, and background. It was symbiotic and complete. Lucille was at the riding center to claim her independence. Fredrico needed someone to fill the void he felt so far from his family. For one hour, each was thoroughly enjoying the other as if they really had something in common.

Lucille understood their relationship. Several grandchildren were close to Fredrico's age. The rider/instructor kinship easily developed into friendship—the first satisfactory one since she lost Irving, and for Frederico, since he left Spain and his own grandmother. Truly, it was not exactly like his own grandmother because *abuela* had to nurture her *nieto*. Lucille Cotton did not have to nurture Fredrico; she only had to be there to make him happy. Fredrico had found the grandmother he missed so much—the beautiful lady back in Spain who had raised him.

Lucille and Fredrico soon found their own world at the riding center. The other riders and teachers in the paddock left them alone. They were oblivious to the other riders anyway.

"I want to do this, but I'm afraid," Lucille explained the first day. Fredrico took her hand and gently took her into the paddock to be close to a horse for the first time in her life.

"He is so big," Lucille whispered. She was thrilled and

excited. Together they led the horse around the paddock with the reins. Lucille followed Fredrico's lead to pet the horse, being careful to show her, with furrowed brow, the places she was not to touch on the horse. She was a quick learner. Then he led her up the mounting stairs.

"Fredrico, I'm scared." She proclaimed.

He gently lifted her onto the saddle as if she had said, *help me on the horse.* He treated her like the most expensive jockey he had ever introduced to a horse he had trained at the track. He took the reins and walked the horse and rider around, flashing a broad smile to give her confidence and tell her she was doing fine.

"Bravo, Lucinda. Bravo."

Soon she was looking forward to mounting the horse while Fredrico walked beside her. Mark had come on the day she first rode the horse around the circle alone with Fredrico on his horse beside her. Mark and Fredrico were extremely proud of her.

🦄 🦄 🦄

Fredrico did not count on Lucille taking him into her family. Pretending not to speak English became a ball and chain and a serious problem. It became a big lie.

Grandma went home, got a Spanish dictionary, and learned how to invite him to lunch. He accepted her invitation to the West Branch Country Club and had a great time watching Grandma tweak her twin grandsons, but he wished now that he had not gone. To reveal that he had understood every word between Grandma and her grandsons would be an insult and would sorely injure their relationship. He genuinely enjoyed being with her and did not want to hurt her in any way. He allowed her to teach him some English. It became more and more difficult to keep up the ruse. Three more weeks and the races would move from Laurel Racetrack to Pimlico in Baltimore. Fredrico would be gone. The problem would fade away.

Fredrico decided he would not accept any more invitations to go out with her, but he did accept her invitations to her home for a sandwich before the lessons. Today that got touchy as Mark came in at lunchtime and ended up at the stable with them.

After Mark took Grandma home from the stables, Fredrico finished his tasks and headed to Sam's for some relaxation. The air was hot and sticky. A beer would go down nicely. The bar was almost empty, and his favorite seat at the far end of the bar was empty. The proprietor knew his preference and put a frosty draft at his spot. "Hi, Nora. What's happening?"

Nora liked to draw him into conversation, see his dark eyes flash, see his wonderful smile, and hear his accent. He was without a doubt the handsomest man frequenting *Sam's* these days.

"Quiet today, Freddy, but it will pick up on Happy Hour. Anything to eat?"

"No, just this and uno to follow."

"You got it!" She went to the opposite end of the bar where Margaret had just settled herself. Freddy noticed her immediately. His day just got more interesting. He sipped his beer and waited for Margaret to get her drink and burger before he picked up his glass and headed for the stool next to her.

"Remember me? " he asked.

"Sure. How's it going?"

"Mind if I join you?"

"I was wondering if you had moved on to Baltimore." She said as he took the seat that she pointed to.

"Not till the 12th of next month. I'm ready to move on. This vagabond life seems to suit me. I love the horses and go where they go."

"This is my hometown. I live about three miles from where I was born. I like to move but I like to come home again."

"Can I buy you another beer? Nora, dos over here!"

"What do you do with the horses?"

"I am a trainer. I make sure I have a healthy horse and that he knows what his job is when the gate opens."

"Are you good at it?"

He loved her directness. "I'm the best." This meeting, unlike the last, was two potential friends getting better acquainted; he laid the ground rules that he wouldn't be around long. She made it clear that this was her turf, and she was comfortable in it. The old pickup lines of the last meeting were gone. The blond slightly aged beauty and the tall, dark young Spaniard soon drew the world around their small space. Each was very interested in the story of the other.

Margaret was fascinated by stories of his homeland and family, especially when he mentioned his grandmother.

"My *abuela*," he told her. "My grandmother, the light in my world."

Freddy was interested in her life in this small town with a matriarch grandmother. Time slipped away.

"My grandmother had dark hair until she was eighty." Freddy started his story. "Her back is straight as a ramrod. She is a pushover for me, but only me. She likes to sit by the fireside and spin stories. She expected a lot from me but allowed me to spend my time at the stables. I went to the university to study business, but it was a waste. I was unhappy to be away from her and the horses. Did you know in Spain your elders can decide for you? We do not have the freedom of choice that you do. She decided my happiness was important and allowed me to go to Madrid to learn to train horses. I studied at the Spanish National Equestrian School in Madrid. I doubt that you have heard of it. Opportunities were better here, and that brought me to the United States and away from her." His voice and face had become sad, but Nora came at the right moment.

"One more?" She asked.

"None for me," they answered in unison.

"My grandmother is the light of our family. She will probably never sit still long enough to spin a story. She wants people to talk about her when she is gone. She did what everyone expected from her for years while her husband and son were alive, but after they died . . . watch out. She was set free. She always said, 'Life is for the living'. Sometimes when she says it now, I think she is saying, 'Life is for living.' I go for both those ideas. She is my role model, but I'm not sure I have as much courage as she. She does things I'm not sure I would be able to do." Talking about grandmothers brought the conversation down, and levity was gone. The new friends were not yet comfortable discussing things close to their hearts. It was time to call it an evening.

"Can we go to dinner Saturday? I mean a real dinner in a Spanish restaurant in Baltimore."

"Freddy, I'm not sure. A family pow-wow. I gotta go pickin'."

"I don't understand. Pow-wow? Picking?" He asked in his charming accent.

"Family meeting, and we kinda pick on each other. We get together to discuss one family crisis after another. My sister is always calling us together for them. This time, it's called by one of my brothers. It might be important. Anyway, I won't know until I check my answering machine at home."

"Can I call you later and see if Saturday might work?" She gave him her number and they walked to the parking lot together.

Nora came to the window to see if they got into separate cars. She loved to follow her customers like this after an interesting pickup. It was the talk in the kitchen at closing time, but there was nothing to talk about tonight. It would have been good gossip. Fredrico so handsome. Margaret, *so* well known, and definitely older—really good gossip. The waitress and cook could mull over his age and her reputation if they had gotten in the same car, but they didn't.

Margaret was happy and contented as she drove up US 1 and made the right on to Whiskey Bottom Road. She paid close attention to the curves because of the beers. Soon, she was on Scaggsville Road and safely in her own driveway. The red light was blinking on the phone. The illuminated number showed nine messages. Margaret hated this machine that she could not live without.

"Beep. 6:32. Maggie, It's Mark. Can you make a family meeting tomorrow at five? We will all be at Sarah's. Let me know... better yet, let Sarah know. See ya."

"Beep. 6:45. Margaret, it's Grandma. I hate talking on these machines. Can you come to my house for dinner tomorrow night? I have a surprise."

"Beep. 7:05. Maggie, Sarah. We have to talk about Grandma again. Mark thinks she is getting ready to take a trip with her riding teacher. Oh, Lord. Pete, Matt, and Jim can't meet tomorrow. How about Saturday at 2? Give me a buzz."

"Beep. 7:16. Maggie, Mark again. Meeting changed. Saturday at 2. Call Sarah."

"Beep. 7:29. Maggie, Sarah. Grandma is inviting us all for dinner tomorrow night. Wonder what that is about. Are you going? "

"Beep. 7:59. It's Grandma. Matt, Pete and John can't make Saturday . . . so can you come on Saturday afternoon? About 2. Love ya, Sweetie."

"Beep. 8:15. Maggie. John here. What the hell is going on? My phone is ringing constantly. Between Sarah's meetings and Grandma's dinner, I haven't a clue. Where are you? Everyone is calling me asking where are you? That's why I don't go to these meetings; they are just like these stupid phone calls. Don't call me back. My phone is off the hook. If Grandma dies, come get me. I have a life."

"Beep. 8:38. Maggie, it's Mark. I have been praying and have decided to cancel the family meeting. I hope you aren't disappointed. Grandma has decided to have her family dinner on Sunday. Looks like everyone can make it except John. We don't know about him; he doesn't answer his phone and turned off his answering machine."

"Beep. 9:12 Maggie. Everything has changed. Give me a call. Where are you? Are you and John together? Can't get him either."

As soon as Margaret got the last message, her phone rang. "Hello?" she said cautiously, expecting another family kook on the line.

"Hello, Margaret. Can we go to Club Madrid with me on Saturday?" That wonderful lyrical Spanish accent came through the phone like a balm.

"I'd go to Madrid with you for dinner Saturday. Baltimore will be great," she yelled.

Chapter 15

Freddy and Margaret

Freddy picked Margaret up at 6:30 on Saturday evening, driving a sleek little green TR3. *Hmmm. The best trainers must make good money,* she thought. She was impressed as she hiked her already short skirt to put her long legs in. He was impressed with that.

"Do you mind the wind? I can put the top up if you prefer."

"I love the wind." She opened her purse and took out a band to pull her hair into a bun. Margaret was always prepared. "Let's go!"

The drive to Baltimore was perfect. The warmth of the day made the breeze just right. His dark hair was blown forward over his forehead and he looked younger. Her blond hair wisped around her face and made her look younger, too. She loved twilight; it hid many years.

Club Madrid was a beautiful restaurant off Pratt Street, heading toward Little Italy. The front was tan stucco with flowers growing from huge planters flanking the door. The faint sound of flamenco music filtered to the sidewalk.

"I hope you like it; it is my new favorite."

Margaret loved it. He finally seemed to be in the right setting as the Matre'd greeted him, "Buena Noches, Fredrico." The waiter immediately provided the finest table and wine. It was obvious he was known here. *Fredrico* was a more fitting name than Freddy. Margaret was not at all surprised when he brushed the menu aside.

"May I order for you?" Without waiting for her answer, he proceeded to give the waiter a spiel in Spanish. It went on for a while, and Margaret began to think she could not possibly eat all he was selecting.

"I have ordered a wonderful wine from the north hills outside of Barcelona. I hope you like seafood. I ordered a dish with shrimp, lobster, crab and clams, and crusty bread. The salad will have a citrus dressing and cheese from the mountains where I live. How does that sound?"

She finally found her voice. "Maravillosa."

"Just wait until you see desert. I love chocolate."

"Me, too."

If it was possible, he was even more handsome in the light and atmosphere of Club Madrid. His language was like music to her. She had been busy using Larry's money to buy whatever she wanted, but she had not been able to buy what she was given to her by Fredrico. Margaret would enjoy this time and place. If it lasted only one hour or two or three, it would be enough. She didn't have to do anything to have it. She didn't have to pay for it, answer for it, or, most of all, ransom it with her body. He was giving it to her. It was free and she was feeling wonderful and freed. Margaret was not sure how she knew that Fredrico was not going to expect her to succumb to him later, but she knew. This was not a seduction. None of the little telltale signs were coming to her. He did not try to stroke her or look into her eyes with some sexual, knowing glance. He took her elbow when he needed to guide her. His smile and laughing eyes were generous . . . not hungry.

"Fredrico, I love it here." He noticed she addressed him by his Spanish name and smiled.

"To our dinner evening." He lifted his glass of Spanish wine to her. "I have told Horatio to take his time with dinner. We want to enjoy the wine first. Ah, here is the cheese. Perfect with this hearty wine."

It was perfect. There was no point in telling him how everything was like stepping into a landscape and finding life perfect on the other side. *He will think I am crazy. Maybe I am,* she thought.

"I have been in the United States for two years now and found no amigo until recently and I have found two. You are one of them. Back in Madrid, I had many amigos. We would find great places to go and share the best food and wine. Until tonight, I have not had an amigo to do that. I think you are looking for a friend, too. We can be great friends." Fredrico's sincerity poured forth.

Margaret saw immediately what he was saying. Why hadn't she seen it before? He was right. She was starving for friendship.

"To friends."

"Amigos." He kissed her hand and promised to take her to see his horses tomorrow. The evening went from fine food to dancing with a marvelous orchestra playing melodies that were new to Margaret but so inviting. He found her a fast learner who could do the intricate Latin steps. Was it the wine or the music that brought her to the floor to dance with several Spanish ladies dancing seductively to the ethnic rhythms? Fredrico led a huge round of applause. Margaret thought she saw lightning.

She learned that Fredrico was more than just a racetrack worker. He obviously had manners and a good upbringing. He knew the fine things of life. Although it crossed her mind to offer to help pay the check, she knew it would be a mistake and an insult to him. She never saw the check come to the table and decided he must have paid while she was in the lady's room.

The next day John saw the picture in the *Baltimore Sun*, City Life section. *Newest, Hottest Night Spot - Club Madrid.* There were four dark-haired beauties dancing with their arms in the air ... and one blond.

"Good golly. That's Maggie!"

Chapter 16

John and Harriet

John and Harriett were as happy as clams; they had found each other and nothing else seemed to matter, so they kept to themselves. Each day, John got stronger. His attitude surely had something to do with that. They sat on the patio and got tans, acting as if they were vacationing in Key West, keeping the feeling going with Jimmy Buffett's *Margaritaville* CD as their constant background. The only person who saw them was the visiting nurse for two days, Harriett sent her away. She simply was not needed.

The happy couple discussed living together, your place or mine. At their age a decision on that was not immediately necessary. Harriett stayed with John at his house but went home about every third day. That worked well for both. They were set in their ways. She had houseplants to tend to, and he had to trim his moustache and clean all those little hairs from the basin. Harriett cooked late summer vegetable dishes and sometimes ordered their favorite pizza. John promised to cook his famous chili and Maryland crab soup as soon as he was able. That was the only promise that went between the new lovers.

He called her Harri, and she called him Dear John.

On wonderful sunny, warm days, the Chesapeake beaconed them. They rode down to Deale and sat on the western bank of the bay to watch the crabbers bring their traps and catches back to the docks. They talked of owning a home on the water and having a dock and boat to enjoy anytime. This talk excited Harri and scared John. Some of his old fears swam in.

One afternoon, as they were catching the late rays, the phone interrupted. "Hello. Sarah! How's it going?"

"Fine here. How about you. Do you need anything? I am going out and thought I would stop by."

"I don't need a thing. My nurse does it all." He winked at Harri. "But, if you want to stop by, Harri and I are just sitting here on the patio having a Marguerita."

Sarah did not want to see him and his boyfriend. "I...I...wanted to talk to you. It will be better when you are alone. Later?"

"Better make it tomorrow morning." Sarah understood what that meant.

The next morning Sarah was there with her bag of problems and two black eyes. He was going to have to concentrate on taking her seriously with her Alvin the Chipmunk look. She forgot her black eyes but noticed John was having trouble keeping a straight face.

"You're looking good, Bro."

"You're looking..." He couldn't go on. He broke into laughter and stammered, "Wh..What happened to you?" Immediately, Sarah remembered her battered eyes and raised her hands to cover them, peeking through the fingers.

" Maggie hit . . . "

He could not wait, "You two had a fight?"

"No. We slipped and her elbow . . . "

"Slipped on what?"

The bathwater. We were in the bath . . . "

"You and Maggie took a bath together?" He could not believe the visual he was getting of these middle-aged sisters bathing together.

"No! Really John! I was taking the bath. The water spilled over when she fell in."

She knew she was not doing a good job of explaining but he kept interrupting the story she had rehearsed for just such an inquisition. If he would just shut up and let her tell it.

"Wait a minute. Maggie banged you with her elbow when she fell into the tub where you were taking a bath."

"No, not while we were in the tub. She tripped over me in the hallway, where I had already slipped on the wet floor. Her elbow got my nose; I thought it was broken. Instead, I got two black eyes. "

"I . . . hahaha . . . hahahah . . . see." John was laughing so hard he had trouble breathing. He put his hand up to stop Sarah from saying anything else; he could not take any more of this story with damaged ribs. It was worse than Chinese laughing torture. Sarah plopped herself down in his easy chair and let her feet go pigeon-toed as she used to do as a child when she didn't know what to do next. She sat and held her chin in her hands, waiting for him to get control as she looked at him with two enormous black holes.

He laughed even harder as he thought she could sing "Swanee." Finally, he got up and got two glasses of water, which helped immensely and gave her a serious case of hiccups. "I have one question. How's Maggie?"

"She (hiccup) has a black eye too. My (hiccup) elbow got her right above the eye when she (hiccup) landed her flip." This was too much; he was laughing again. This time the black-eyed, pigeon-toed girl was hiccupping loudly and gulping water, which everyone knows will not take away the spasms of the diaphragm.

"Sarah, You know people will think Tom did this."

"Yes (hiccup), I know, but I haven't been around (hiccup) anyone and if you are any indication of what to expect(hiccup) from family, it would be easier letting strangers (hiccup) think I am a battered wife." She got up and went into the kitchen to eat a spoonful of sugar, which finally took away the hiccups.

"I'm sorry, Sis. But it is a good story." He went over and gave her a hug. "What's on your mind today?"

"John, I know you hate these family matters, but I think since you keep yourself away from them so well, you could give an objective opinion. What are we going to do about Grandma?"

"I can give you my opinion without even knowing what is on your mind."

She leaned back in the chair, folded her hands in her lap, and waited. John got her body language and the hurt she was feeling. "Sarah, let it go. Whatever Grandma is doing or wants to do, let it happen. It is going to happen no matter what you do. You want what is best for her, and so do I, but has it ever occurred to you that we may not *know* what is best for her?"

"Yes, it has, as a matter of fact. I may act like I am sure of what I do, but often I am unsure . . . but I know my motives. I want her safe, and I want her around for a long time."

"Of course. but you cannot assure that for yourself or anyone else, no matter how you love them. No one was able to keep Mom and Dad home the night they died. If they had stayed home, they would never have seen Merle Haggard in person at the Grand Ole Opry. How many times did Dad say, 'I want to see Merle before I die?'"

"That's true but Mom didn't care about seeing him and she died too."

"What's your point?" He asked.

Sarah shrugged. She didn't have a point. "Let me ask you one question. Would you stand by and watch Grandma go to Spain with her riding instructor?"

"That is a good question." John took time to think and answer because he knew Sarah would bring his words back to him, and they had better be right.

"I would want to know him. I would want to know the plans, including the return flight. But I would not try to keep her from going."

"Do you think the others would feel the same way? Am I so far wrong on this?"

"Sarah, you are thinking of Grandma as you think of four-year-old Amanda. Grandma is not a child. Her limitations are really only physical—stamina. A young companion will help her. I believe Maggie, Jim, and Pete will feel as I do. Maybe Mark, but he can only measure the abstract. If Regina were here, she would buy the ticket and drive the old girl to the airport. Are you so sure she is going to Spain with this . . . riding instructor?"

"She is up to something but I'm not sure. I worry about her health, but she would not take a trip if she were ill. Would she?"

"Why not ask her?" This strange idea had not crossed Sarah's mind. "I tell you what, I'll go to the phone right now and ask her outright."

"Ask her what?"

"Are you going to Spain . . . and are you sick . . . if you want me to."

"No. No." that was too direct for poor Sarah.

"I'll ask her to invite Fredrico to the dinner. If we don't find out what is going on, you can ask your questions then. Grandma is having a family dinner on Sunday. I think I will ask her to invite him. Pete and Will have already met him."

"That sounds like a plan." She got up to go and noticed a new arrangement on the table. "Nice."

"Harri's special touch," he said lovingly.

"How's your hip?" Sarah quickly went to another subject.

"It's coming along great. Notice. I'm not using the cane at home, but I do take it when I go out."

"Suppose Grandma falls and breaks her hip like you did? While she's in Spain?"

"I'll tell you what. If she does, I'll fly to Spain to take care of her and even take you and Harri with me."

That little threesome did not interest Sarah, but she liked the idea of John taking some responsibility. She grasped the thread of an offer that he made.

"Funny thing," she said, "I've always wanted to go to Spain."

"You're a looker, Sarah. Maybe you should put the move on the riding instructor, and you would get there. But wait for those eyes to clear up." Sarah finally had to laugh at this off-sided compliment. She loves her brother, even if he is gay.

"Better yet," she said, "let's send Maggie in to distract him."

As she walked out the door, John touched her arm, "Sarah, Grandma has always enjoyed life. If she wants to do something out from under our umbrella, we should not try to stop her. She never put the damper on any of us. I would suggest a Marguerita."

"For Grandma?'

"For you. See you Sunday."

Chapter 17

Sarah and Fredrico

"It looks like everyone is coming to dinner even John," Sarah told Tom. "He never comes to these family things. I can't help but wonder how it will go?"

"Lord, Sarah, I don't know. I don't even try to figure your family. You think Grandma's dying and Mark thinks she is going to run off with some Spaniard. I must say, I'm looking forward to this gathering; should be fun. More fun than your usual family dinners."

Sarah was sitting at the dressing table looking at her reflection in the mirror. Her eyes had passed from the black stage to shades of purple and yellow. Her big green eyes centered amid all that color made a double kaleidoscope or one of those pinwheel suckers the grandchildren get at the fair. "I'm trying to put some more make up on my eyes. Who would have thought a blow to the nose would make me look like this." She was thinking her sister always got the best of any deal. Margaret's black eye was across the lid. She could hide it with eye shadow.

Make-up only made Sarah's eyes look stranger. She refused to take Tom's advice and tell everyone what happened. "You look fine, Sweetheart." He lied to his wife hoping to get extra close in bed tonight. He leaned down and kissed her and rubbed her back, so she knew exactly what was on his mind.

"Tom, get the phone." She was saved by the bell.

"Hello? Hi Grandma."

"Sure, we can do that. Really? Ok. See you at two."

"Grandma wants us to bring extra folding chairs. Seems like John and Maggie are bringing dates."

"Ohhhh, Tom." Sarah was starting a tailspin. Tom knew the signs. Just when everything seemed to be going well. He would be lucky to get her settled down in time to go to Grandma's. Romance tonight went out the window. "John is bringing Harry; I just know he is."

"So? Come on Sarah. What if he is bringing his boyfriend? We are all adults here. You don't have a problem with George and Maurice."

"But neither one of them is my brother."

"Sarah, stop making a problem where there is none."

"What about Grandma. She won't be able to handle this. She **is** of the old school."

"You underestimate Grandma." Tom was quick to point out. "Sometimes she is ahead of us all."

Sarah ignored Tom's remark and held on to her conviction that she should get a plan to protect Grandma. "It's thoughtless of John to spring his gay partner on everyone at Grandma's today. We are going early. Get a couple of bottles of wine from the cabinet. We will pour some to keep everyone mellow," Sarah directed.

"Well, that's the smartest thing you have said today." Tom

patted her butt and went to the wine rack. Sarah and Tom headed over to Grandma's with chairs and wine to get the dinner party going. They were surprised to see two cars already parked in her drive. They went in to find strangers in the kitchen.

"Where is Grandma?" Sarah demanded. "And why are you cooking in her kitchen?"

"I'm in here darlin'." Grandma came from the front room. "I want you to meet my friends from the wine club. They aren't staying for dinner, but they came to help me cook. Jack and Gloria, this is my granddaughter Sarah and her husband, Tom."

"Pleased to meet you. The paella is coming together. Doesn't it smell wonderful?"

Sarah looked at Tom with a 'what-happened-to good-ole-pot-roast' look. "Yes, it does. "

"It has clams, fish and sausage, and it goes well with white and red wine. My friends helped me chose wines from Spain. Besides suiting the dish, they are appropriate for the occasion."

"Who's coming and what is the occasion? You have a lot of places."

Let's see." Grandma said. "You and Tom, Mark and Pam, Jim and Marge, Pete and Syl, Matt, by himself, of course, John and Harri, Margaret and a friend. I don't know his name. Oh . . . and my special guests are Fredrico and Doc Belford."

Sarah decided to ignore the mention of Fredrico's name. "Doc Belford? That is a nice surprise. And the occasion?"

"Doc is here to help with the announcement I am to make. Sarah, what is wrong with your eyes? You look like a raccoon."

"I had a little accident. Fell on a slippery floor and hit my nose. I never thought it would give me two black eyes. Is it that noticeable? I put extra make-up on."

"Well, child, That's exactly how you look—two black eyes covered with make-up. If I didn't know Tom better, I'd think you were battered. Best if you don't go around strangers. They will look at Tom funny." With shaking hands Sarah took the wine that Tom had opened and poured some into a drinking glass. While Grandma was fussing with the crusty bread, Sarah gave Tom the high sign that she needed to talk to him on the back porch.

"I told you. I knew it." She started right in. "How am I going to make it through this dinner? John is bringing Harry, and you heard her—Fredrico is coming too. I know exactly what is going to happen here today!"

"What are you getting at?" Tom was exasperated with his wife.

"You heard what she said. She needs Doc here to make her announcement and the wine from Spain must mean she is going to Spain with that . . . that   . . . riding Spaniard! It is worse than I thought"

Grandma popped her head out the door. "Margaret called, her friend can't come. One less chair, Tom."

" I'm beginin' to look forward to meeshing Harry. Pour me more swine . . . I'm gonna skip Spain and stick with Calli-for-nee." He smiled at his dear wife who could not drink and talk; never could. They came back into the kitchen where Pete was talking about John.

"I'm glad John is coming today. It has been a long time since we were all together."

"Yes, maybe it is his new friend, Harri influenced him. He needs someone in his life. I couldn't be happier for him. I met Harri at the hospital," Grandma announced

"Grandma, you approve of them as a couple? This is a different choice for him, unlike the others." Pete offered.

"Yes, and I guess that is why I approve. He has had enough of those young, flighty women. Now he has someone with real strength, more like him," Grandma spoke her piece.

The men just looked at each other as Sarah's mouth dropped open and a trickle of wine dripped down her chin. Grandma was more in tune with the modern age than they could have imagined.

All she could say was, "If Harry's OK with you, I gesh I have to agree."

"Well, the bottom line is if John wants Harri and if that will get him back into the family fold . . . how wonderful is that? I want to see all of my grandchildren happy before I die."

Sarah began to whimper and cry drunken tears that poured down her face, washing the heavy makeup around her eyes.

"All this advice from you and John to *just let her go.*" Sarah whispered to Tom as she struck him in the chest like he was her enemy.

Christ, no sex again tonight. These Cotton's are literally unscrewing my life, Tom thought, as Sarah pulled away from the embrace he offered for her pain.

"Well, Sarah, leave it to you to read all of that in what Grandma said You make it sound like you are expecting Zorro to come in here and steal your grandmother . . .and carve a Z in the chocolate cake. Drink your wine," was his only suggestion.

"I am so tired of do-nothing-men! *Just let her go. It will be alright.* Well, it *won't* be alright." Sarah was pacing up and down the porch and drinking the wine as if she was dying of thirst and had finally reached the oasis. Tom refilled her glass. It was drained when she turned on her heels to face her husband. "If she leafs tomorrow, today is the las' time any offus will see her!" Sarah knew she was slurring her words. She pulled herself together to say with utter clarity, "What do you say to that? Just let her go?' Tom was refilling the glass as she made one more pass across the porch.

Sarah took a long draw of the wine. Tom went over to her and took her into her arms. The wine made it possible for her to accept his embrace.

"Hon, stop doing this to yourself. No one else is trying to second guess; I wish you wouldn't either. Drink your wine." In less than seven minutes, Sarah had finished her California Kool-Aid and was worrying less and less. Her tears made trails of Mississippi mud coming from the black delta of her eyes. What a sight! Fortunately, everyone was busy greeting a handsome Spanish man coming through the back door.

"Pronto?" he asked in his thick Latin accent.

"Perfect time, Fredrico. You know Pete and Will. This is Sarah and Tom."

Sarah put down the dishtowel that had been mopping up the muddy flood on her face. She extended her hand. With dashing charm, he smiled, took it, and kissed it. "Encantada."

Sarah forgot she looked like a Mardi Gras mistake as he was looking into her eyes and winning her over. His gallantry hid the slightest hint that he thought she was a strange looking doll.

Tom shook his hand, gave a nod, and smiled. His glance told Fredrico that he was welcome to the fun of this kitchen full of crazy family.

"How's the English?" Pete inquired.

"Better, gracias." Fredrico had come early hoping to have a chance to talk to Lucille and make his confession before the others arrived. He wanted to explain why he had lied about speaking English. After a lifetime of using his good looks and polished ways for conquests, he had finally found two women that he cared about, and he didn't want to hurt either one by being less than honest. "How come you know Fredrico?" Tom was addressing his brother-in-law. "He has been a mystery man to us."

"Grandma brought him to the lunch at West Branch one day, weeks ago." Pete explained. "Yes, the day before John broke his hip."

"Mark came to watch me ride one day, and he met Fredrico, too. He is not a mystery man." Grandma added

"Come, Fredrico. Open the Spanish wine." Tom handed him a bottle.

"Oh, Modesto. Delighted." He was glad to have a job and be out of the hot seat. As he worked on pulling the cork with the latest gadget from the wine shop, he noticed Sarah watching him unabashedly. He looked down at the task and back, and she had not diverted her eyes. "Modesto wine?" he asked as she extended her empty glass with a shaking hand. *She's drunk.* he thought as he filled her glass and turned to fill the glasses Grandma had set before him.

"Sarah, may I sit here with you?" Fredrico asked.

"Slure, Fredco." She slid over on the window seat, and he sat beside her. Sarah knew this would be difficult, but with all her strength, she pulled herself together. She knew she was slurring her words, but with great concentration, she could say what she wanted. "Are you going for Spain?"

Fredrico thought maybe his English was not good on prepositions. "No, I came from Spain."

'Where are you going next?"

"Pimlico."

"Is that Spain or Mex-she-co." It sounded Spanish to her.

"That is in Baltimore."

"Baltimore, Maryland?"

"Yes."

You are taking Grandma to Baltimore?"

Now Fredrico was confused, although he had lots of experience talking to drunks. "If she wants to go, I could."

"No, you can't!" Sarah downed her Modesto and lowered her voice to an emphatic whisper. "I won't let you take her, and don't you forget it You . . . you . . . Don Juan." She got up and stumbled. Fredrico steadied her so she could reach the stair railing just beside the window. "Tom!" she called. "I am going up to resh." Tom thought that was a very good idea. He helped her up the stairs and onto the closest bed.

Chapter 18

The Cottons Gather

Freddy called Margaret early Sunday morning.
"Margarite, Dear, I cannot go with you today to meet your family, I have another engagement. So sorry."

"I'm disappointed."

"Me, too. Can I see you in this evening?" He invited.

That helped with the disappointment. Margaret would see him later.

It was hard enough to get everyone into Grandma's house and endure the togetherness required at one of these Sunday dinners without some special diversion. Freddy would have certainly supplied that. Even now, as she thought about him, her pre-menopause hormonal temperature rose.

Later, she dialed Grandma's number with no enthusiasm.

"Hi, Grandma. Who's there?"

"Well, they are arriving as we speak. Sarah, Tom, Jim, Marge, and my riding teacher, so far.

"My friend can't come; he has another commitment. I will be a little late. Go ahead with dinner, but I will be there.'

"Oh, I forgot, Doc Belford is here, too. You had better hurry; we will not start without you. We are serving wine and, there is to be an announcement later. That has already put Sarah into a tailspin. Pete and Sylvia are here now. Matt can't be far behind."

"I'll be there, but I don't need any pot roast." Margaret never forgot those size four miniskirts in the closet.

"No pot roast today, Margaret. An all-Spanish meal, and we are not starting without you. Hurry up!" Grandma hung up the phone and returned to her guests.

"Good for the old girl! I guess she is going to take that trip. I better get there to cheer her on." Margaret talked to herself and headed for the shower. She chose a pair of stretch pants and a big oversized Irish linen shirt. With her hair done in a ponytail at the nape of her neck, she looked very young, especially from a distance. Margaret even rushed a little bit and forgot the disappointment that had slowed her down just an hour ago. She wanted to join the fun when Grandma finally told everyone what she wanted to do. Margaret hurried off feeling confident that Fredrico would brighten her evening.

£ £ £

The yard was full of cars, and the chatter from the house was spilling onto the porch. Margaret was happy; she loved this family and looked forward to whatever nonsense that would come from this gathering. Tom was the first to get to her. "Maggie, would you go upstairs to the front room and get Sarah ready to come down? She had some wine ... and well, you know."

"I get the picture." Margaret took the stairs and went up without going in to greet everyone.

'Sarah, are you awake?"

"Is it over?" Sarah mumbled in the pillow.

"It hasn't started yet. I just got here and came to get you." She lifted the shade and looked at her sister. "Good God, Sarah!" Margaret was looking back at her in a mask of purple, green, yellow and black. The bruises around her eyes and the colors of healing were the colors that fly on every lamppost in New Orleans. The black mascara running down her face gave her the look of a bayou witch. Margaret was never good at hiding her feelings and so, she laughed.

"What . . . what's so funny?" Sarah asked.

"Let me wash your eyes and repair your face. No, no . . . you don't want to see." She stopped Sarah from rising and looking for a mirror. "Stay right there; I will get a cloth." Margaret headed to the bathroom to get away from Sarah and take the opportunity to really laugh while the running water hid her insensitivity to her sister's plight. "I can't believe how long those black eyes have lasted. It's been almost a week."

"Geez, I know."

Margaret went to work to make Sarah presentable and did a good job; she was an artist with an abundant supply of make-up in her purse. Sarah looked better but still had circles around her eyes; nothing could take them away, but with lighter make-up, rouge, and lipstick, she looked acceptable.

"Come on Sis, let's go down and have some fun."

"Grandma's boyfriend is down there, and I'm sure they are going to Spain together."

"I hope they do. Now get your ass downstairs and smile.

Maybe no one will look at your eyes."

Sarah was tired of being alone. She would do as Margaret said. The wine left her mellow and agreeable. They descended the stairs into the warm and wonderfully aromatic kitchen just as John and Harri came in.

"Sarah and Maggie! Meet Harri. Harriet these are my sisters." John introduced, and stepped forward to give each sister a hug. Harri offered her hand. With John's chatter about her being his nurse, Harriett didn't notice that neither sister could say a word. She did notice that their mouths were hanging open seeming to needed outside help to close them. John and Harriett moved into the dining room before Sarah and Margaret exchanged looks and broke into gales of laughter. They were still laughing and marveling at John's love when Matt stepped into the doorway with his friend, Charles.

"Maggie, Sarah, this is Charles Chambers. Charles, my sisters, Margaret and Sarah." Charles extended a limp wrist and gentle, smooth hand for the girls to squeeze.

"Pleased to meet you, Charl..." Margaret started her greeting.

"Please call me Charles," he interrupted. "I'm pleased to meet you, too."

"Charles," she spoke his name with warmth and understanding.

Matt looked stressed as he spoke quietly to his sisters, "Step out here on the porch with us." Matt and Charles backed up; Margaret and Sarah took two steps forward—a slow Cha Cha Cha, "Please help me to introduce Charles into the family. He is my ... um ... significant other. We are ... together." It was difficult to find word for something he had never explained before. Matt reached for Sarah's hand. "I need your help to get over this hurdle."

"Charles is your boyfriend?" Margaret didn't mince any words. Her quick observation saw a gentle, attractive, well-dressed man, just the right age for Matt. She noted he was quick to smile, and his deep and beautiful baritone voice belied his sexual preferences. He slowly slipped his arm around Matt's waist; there was no doubt. Charles' arm seemed to give Matt strength. Margaret picked up the doubt in her brother's eyes as she placed her hand on his arm. *No hurdles,* she thought and hoped that it was true.

"You mean like boyfriend—boyfriend?" That was all that Sarah could say. She could hardly process this with her emotions raging and a high blood alcohol level.

"Yes. Charles and I are a couple. Today, I are living in the open. Out of the closet, as they say."

"Welcome to the family, Charles." Margaret gave Matt a big, sincere hug. Then she did the same for Charles. She could see the relief come over both faces. Maybe this would be easier than Matt told Charles it would be.

"There will be no hurdles. Your sisters will lead." Margaret would do what Sarah, frozen in time and lost in a fog, could not do. "Let's go in. Dinner is ready. I'll make introductions. "What's your last name again, Charles?"

"Thanks, Maggie. His name is Charles Chambers...but I'll make the introductions."

Maggie gave them a big smile and pushed open the door while pulling Sarah's sleeve to get her back into the world.

Although Sarah was aware of the happy relief on her beloved brother's face, she could hardly breathe. Her mind jumped to one thought—*does Pete know what his twin is about to do?*

At that moment, Grandma came to the door to see why her

grandchildren were on the porch instead of in the dining room. "I'm counting heads. Who is out here? Sarah, Margaret, Matt and …

"Grandma, this is Charles." Matt spoke up. "Charles Chambers."

"How do you do, Charles. Welcome. You can have the place we set for Margaret's friend since she is alone." Margaret enjoyed this effort by Grandma to pair her up for dinner. However, Matt was not about to let that happen.

"Grandma, Charles is my partner. Do you know what that means?"

"It doesn't mean anything to me, Matt. You are welcome to bring your friend or partner or whatever into my house. Charles, you are welcome, as I said before." Grandma smiled and took his elbow. "Do you like paella?"

"Yes, ma'am," Charles responded in a deep, rich, sultry Southern voice. He liked Grandma immediately and felt he had passed another hurdle, but he hadn't met Pete yet.

"Good. As soon as the rice is done and Mark gets here, we will eat. I hope you like wine. Tell me, Charles, do you live with Matt?" She held onto Charles' elbow and led him into the house negating the requirement that the question be answered by Matt or Charles. Inside the door, she announced, " Tom, bring the chair back. Matt's friend, Charles, will take the extra place."

Margaret lifted Sarah's elbow and placed it in Matt's hand so they could steady each other as they walked into the house. Margaret needed no help; she was having too much fun. *John is straight, and Matt is gay!* Her mind played with these intriguing facts. Now Sarah and the whole family can come into the real world, where not everyone fits in the same mold. Just as she was about to enter the house Mark and Pam arrived.

"Hey Maggie!"

"Mark and Pam. The party has started. You have already missed a lot."

"Really? Is everyone here?" Mark asked.

"I haven't even been in to see everyone yet, but Grandma said when you arrived, we would eat, so I guess you are the last ones. Let's go in. Doc Belford is here, so is Grandma's riding instructor ... and Matt has a friend with him."

"Mark, how do you feel about Grandma going off on a trip?"

"I think it would be great for her. Is she going?"

"I don't know, but her riding instructor is here. We are having a Spanish meal, and she is serving a great Spanish wine. I think this family can come together on this and be happy for whatever she decides she wants to do."

"Even Sarah?"

"Even Sarah. By the way, don't say anything about Sarah's black eyes."

Mark turned to Pam and mouthed, "Black eyes?" Each shrugged and entered the kitchen of the little house on A Street. The party was complete.

Scattered through the house, the family was enjoying fine imported cheeses and crackers along with the wine Tom poured. The dining room table had been stretched into the living room where the drop leaf table extended it even further. Grandma was determined to seat everyone together, and Margaret found a job spreading the cloth and setting the table. The headcount was now fourteen. John came forward to help Margaret.

"Where's Tom?" Margaret asked, knowing he needed to attend to Sarah.

"He is on the front porch with the riding instructor, waiting to be called to eat. Have you met him yet?" Margaret was placing the last plates on the table.

"No. Here, set the knives, forks, and spoons by the plates." Margaret began setting the table with John's help. They did the job and chatted.

"Have you met Charles?" The napkins were placed beside the plates.

"No." The water glasses were to the right of the knives. "Who is this Charles?" The wine glasses were put next to the water glasses.

"He is Matt's partner." The salad plates full of greens and tomatoes were at the left of the forks

"Matt's partner as in partner, partner?" Salt and peppers were placed on each table.

"You got it. Sarah worried about the wrong brother." The butter dishes were alongside the salt and pepper.

"What do you mean 'the wrong brother'" John asked,

"She thought Harri was a man. At the hospital you asked for Harry the toupee, and it seemed you were asking for your boyfriend, Then Harri helped with your recovery and the pot thickened."

"Oh my god! You've gotta be kidding"

"Sarah lost some sleep over you, John."

"Can't wait to tell Harri all about this. She will get a good idea what this family is like."

"Look at Grandma; she likes Charles. I'm sure we all will, except Pete." Hot pads were placed for the paella. The table was set.

"Tom, come in and pour the wine for the table. We are serving another Spanish wine from Grandma's wine cellar." Sarah was beginning to sound like her old self but did not steady enough to help Margaret with glasses or wine.

Tom and Fredrico came in from the porch.

Margaret dropped the wine bottle she was holding and looked into the eyes of Grandma's riding instructor. Neither said a word of greeting. A big red spill spread on Grandma's carpet. Margaret's eyes never dropped to see it. She was frozen in a stare with Fredrico.

"Now, now, Margaret. Don't be upset. The bottle was almost empty. Nothing can spoil this good time. Tom, blot it, and I will call a rug cleaner tomorrow. Let's eat." Grandma took charge of assigning seats, only mindful of boy-girl as much as possible, around the table, not caring if it was spouses. She pointed around the table. "Doc, John, Sarah, Mark, Sylvia, John, Margaret, Tom, Pam, Harri, Pete, Sylvia, Matt, Charles, Fredrico, and me. She made sure Doc was on her left and Fredrico was on her right. It was her party and there it would be her choice as to who had those seats of honor. Margaret moved to her seat like a robot.

"Wait, I did something wrong; I have two men together," pointing to Matt and Charles. "Oh well, we are a little short on women! There is no need to move around; it is too congested. You don't mind sitting with each other, do you?" Matt did not look up as he shook his head from side to side.

"Before my friends bring this wonderful Spanish meal from the kitchen, I want to be sure everyone has met Fredrico and Charles. Fredrico is my riding instructor, and Charles is Matt's guest. We are so happy to have Doc Belford here, and Margaret, I am sorry your friend could not come today."

"He's here." She said under her breath, unheard in the riotous assembly.

Chapter 19

Cotton Pickin'

"Mark, the blessing, please."

"Heavenly Father, your blessings are beyond measure to this family. We are so grateful for this time together and the gathering of family and friends. We ask a special blessing on Grandma for all she does for each of us. We ask that you bless Regina, who could not be with us. Please stay with us as we take our different paths, never forgetting that we are part of this family and Your family, too. Bless this food to nourish our bodies and us to your service. Amen."

The cooks began to set steaming platters of paella, rice, and wonderful seafood on the table, along with baskets of warm crusty bread.

Tom rose to propose a toast. "To Grandma." Around the table, glasses were raised to the one thing they could all agree on. "To the example you are to us ... generous, loyal, loving and gracious. You are beautiful and the greatest blessing in this family. Here. Here."

The food was wonderful and the conversation lively, but due to the length of the table, confined to whichever end you were seated. The platters were passed twice, the bread broken, and the wine poured. No one seemed to miss the pot roast. No one noticed that Margaret and the riding instructor had no appetite for the traditional dish of Spain.

Tom kept the wine glasses full, and all agreed that the special wine was excellent except Charles who passed his glass to Margaret. "I don't drink."

"Before we have dessert, we are going to have a Cotton Pickin'." Grandma announced. All the siblings would have to speak. It was a command.

Margaret asked for more wine, "Please." She passed her empty glass to Tom.

"Why don't you start, Grandma?" suggested Pete.

"Just let me say how happy I am that you are all here. After everyone picks cotton, I will bale it up. The Cotton I pick to start is Sarah."

Food in her stomach helped Sarah to sober up. She managed to speak clearly with great concentration. "I'm a cotton pickin' black-eyed beauty tonight. I just want you to know that Tom didn't do this to me..." she pointed to her colorful eyes...," Maggie did. She loves to tell the story. Ask her. It was an accident. Maybe I deserve black eyes because I have been a donkey, to put it politely, at the dinner table. I'd like to promise I won't be so stubborn and bossy in the future, but you know me better than that!" She drew a breath and called on Matt.

"I'm cotton pickin' gay. Charles and I . . . well you know. He is part of this family now. I hope you will welcome him and get to know him." Matt and Charles exchanged looks of relief.

"Sometimes it takes a long time to know yourself. Finally and happily, I have come to like the person I am. The only thing we, Charlie and I, need is the chances to gather with you like this... and live our good life." Matt spoke emotionally and without breathing. He quickly noted the receptive expressions on the faces of his family. "The Cotton I pick is John."

"Hold, hold it." Pete interrupted, coming to his feet. "Are you saying you are homosexual?"

"Yes. Have you got a good attorney's argument against that?" Matt answered, rising from his seat.

"No, but by God, now we are no longer identical! You are just another cotton pickin' sibling." With that, Pete and all around the table broke into laughter and applause and that relieved the air of tension that had whispered in the room a moment ago.

Grandma got from her seat to give Matt the hug that he needed at that moment.

"Pete, you went out of turn. John was called. Are you going to pick cotton or pass it to him?" Grandma directed.

"While I have the floor, let me just say...." A lawyer rarely yields the floor. "...Charles, relax. We hope you feel welcome here. You are. I am sure everyone agrees." Pete walked around the table to shake hands with Matt and Charles. "John, back to you."

John stood and put his hand on Harriett's shoulder. "Matt isn't the only one with an announcement. Not the only one bringing someone new to the family. I'm a cotton pickin' bald head, about-to-be-wed." He paused just long enough for his words to sink in. "Harri has accepted my proposal and ring. Just thinking about you (he looked straight at Grandma) gave us the courage to do what we want to do. We will tie the knot at the courthouse privately. We don't want a Cotton commotion there, but we'll arrange a celebration after." He bent down to give Harri a kiss. "I have given up my toupee for her. How about a toast to my beautiful, wonderful bride-to-be?" Harriett stood beside John. They beamed happiness, as the table burst into applause again.

"Hear, hear. A toast to hairless John and beautiful Harri. Wishing you all the best. Welcome to the family, Harriet." offered Mark.

"The Cotton I pick is Jim," John finished and sat down.

"I'm a cotton pickin' happy man. Marge and I have adopted a healthier lifestyle. We go to the gym twice a week. I don't have a black eye, a boyfriend, or a bald head . . . but I sure enjoy all your accomplishments." The table broke out in laughter one more time. It had turned into a rousing celebration. "The Cotton I pick is Mark."

"I'm a cotton pickin' wiser man. I've had a great career and traveled the world. I've studied international relationships and been baffled by these on A Street."

"You and me too," offered Jim. "I'm sorry, Mark. I didn't mean to interrupt your pickin,"

Mark resumed, "I've seen many amazing sights around the world. And people who could rule countries. But the person that impresses me most is Grandma, straight and proud, in the saddle on that horse. Absolutely amazed me. Almost for the first time, I knew what an amazing, capable, strong woman she has always been and will always be. I don't have everything figured out; I don't have to have all the answers . . . but she taught me the value of a flannel shirt and a little gold cross pinned there," he said as he patted the cross on his pocket. Thank you, Grandma. God Bless us, everyone." Mark sat down. "Maggie. Your turn, Sis."

Margaret rose for her turn. She straightened the hair that had loosened from her ponytail, pinched her cheeks to heighten the color. She moved as if she were on stage and the lights had just come up. When she knew she was just right, she began. "Pay attention. I can hardly explain but here goes. Grandma has a riding instructor, Fredrico. I have a wonderful boyfriend, Freddy. They were going to meet each other here tonight, but it turns out they are each other." Maggie gave them a moment. "Fredrico. Freddy! Go figure. It could be that Grandma and I are dating the same man. Don't that just put a clam in your paella pan?"

This was happening fast, and most did not get exactly what Margaret was saying, but Fredrico and Grandma were following her perfectly. It could have been a tense moment, but Margaret was smiling broadly. Usually she was an observer, watching her crazy family. Now the stage was hers, and she wondered how her own personal drama would play out. Grandma had a quizzical look on her face. Fredrico looked like he could bolt from the table at any moment. Margaret was not going to let that happen and went like lightning, almost tripping on Snow White, to get to his side. She pushed her hair back and looked into Freddy's wonderful face.

"Fredrico, are you my Freddy?" She did not want an answer. She wanted to kiss him. While everyone else's mouths were hanging open, Freddy returned Margaret's kiss.

Fredrico rose fully composed and addressed Grandma. "May I speak, Lucinda?"

"Of course," Grandma answered. She and everyone around the table wanted to hear what the Spaniard had to say, especially Sarah who had suspended her wine drinking.

"Lucinda," he addressed her with a slight bow. He pulled Margaret close and slipped his hand around her waist. They were an astoundingly beautiful couple, smiling and standing tall. "I am Fredrico Del Lancio." He did a slight bow. "Thank you for having me here to be with your family. First, I want to apologize to you and Pete, Matt, and Mark. I am very sorry that I let you believe I did not know English. It was an innocent lie to help Lucinda . . . Pardon, I call your grandmother Lucinda. I told the lie to help her learn to ride. It got out of hand when she set about making me a part of her family."

Everyone around the table understood this truth.

"None of my students ever did that before. You see, she kept telling me she couldn't ride and was afraid of the horse, so I pretended I didn't understand. She overcame her fear. She is a wonderful rider. Mark saw her on the horse. My wish is that you all could." He walked away from Margaret to kiss Grandma's hand.

Fredrico did not sit down. Instead, he took Margaret's hand and invited her to stand with him. "Margarite. I have never lied to you; I just didn't know Lucinda was your grandmother. When I saw you here today, I was overjoyed. It was too good to be true." He lifted his drink to toast her but couldn't speak; her lips were planted where he would have formed the words. She pulled his chair back, pushed him into the seat, and sat on his lap again as if to say, *so there!*

"It's your turn, Grandma!" Margaret happily turned the attention away from herself and Fredrico.

"First, let's have some more wine. Tom, fill the glasses," It was Sarah ordering the wine.

"I will sit while I pick my cotton. You have given me many bales to carry tonight, along with the joy of having all of you here with special friends. First, as always, I toast Irving and your parents, Patrick and Joanne. And another toast to Regina, always somewhere else. In Africa, now. To them all!" Everyone lifted their glasses with tears in their eyes. "Next, I toast the Cotton spouses, Pam. Marge, Sylvia, plus Harriet—and significant other, Charles—for putting up with this little game we play. I am sure you are happy not to be born into this family, but I pray that you are happy to be a part of it!" A pause was taken to lift the glasses again to let the wine do more mellowing.

"Now, I am going to make my announcement." She went to the sideboard and grabbed a small sombrero and castanets. In a flash, she was a flamingo dancer with her hands clicking out a Latin rhythm. Her eyes were dancing, her colorful dress and hat took away years, Grandma became a senorita.

"I am going to take the trip I have always wanted to take. I am going to Spain. Thanks to the books Sarah brought me and the things I have learned about Spain from Fredrico, I have decided that is where I would love to go." She removed the hat and took her seat to emphasize her seriousness.

"I'll go with you, Grandma," called Sarah.

"No. I don't want you to go, Sarah. Or any of you." Sarah closed her mouth and tried to hang on to her own words of moments ago. She was in danger of being a donkey's ass again.

"Freddy, are you taking my grandmother to Spain? Is that where you are going next week?" Margaret asked.

"I am not taking Lucinda anywhere, although it would be

a great pleasure to show my country to such a fine lady." His accent charmed the women and irritated the men. "She should see the glory of Madrid, the bullfights. I have told her of the marvelous seashore. However, I am not going to Spain; I am going to Pimlico. The race meet opens there on the 12th."

"Thank you, Federico. Margaret, I am surprised. You would be the last one I would expect to come up with the wild idea that I was running away with Federico."

"Oh, it wasn't my idea, Grandma. That idiocy came from Sarah . . . but you did steal my hair color, and I guess you could steal my boyfriend if you had a mind to." Her levity was not lost on the diners. "All kidding aside, you can't take Fredrico, and you shouldn't go alone. You must have a good plan." Margaret suggested.

"Ok, I'm still pickin' cotton. As I was trying to say...I am going to Spain, and my traveling companion will be Doc Belford. Will you allow me to change the game a little and pick on Doc even though he is not a Cotton?"

Dr. Belford rose and patted Grandma's hand.

"It wasn't easy, but I have convinced your grandmother to allow me to escort her to Spain. I am fully retired now. It seemed like a perfect idea. I hope you will think so, too. We are booked to leave Thursday a week, in eleven days. Our return ticket is not dated. Our return ticket is open in case we want to continue to other places after the tour in Spain ends. Our tour group caters to seniors so the pace should fit us very well. Any questions? Oh, and we have separate rooms at all hotels in case you are worried about intimacy."

"If I were worried about intimacy, having separate rooms would not satisfy me. We have all had a considerable amount of intimacy outside of bedrooms! I really don't want to have this discussion in front of grandma let alone *about* grandma." Margaret was again taking the spotlight with her candor.

Doc smiled and continued. "She isn't going without your approval. What do you say?"

Margaret, "Yea"

Mark, "Yea"

John, "Alright with me"

Matt and Pete, in unison, "Have a great time."

John, "Send me a card."

Sarah, "Go. . . . We will miss you." She was trying very hard not to be an ass.

"I talked to Regina last night, and she is going to meet us in Spain at the end of the month. So, I thank you all for your approval. But I have to be honest, I was going no matter what you said. Doc is just being nice."

"Nothing like having a doctor along on a trip," said John.

"He is not going as my doctor but as my very long-time and dear friend." One by one, they walked around so each could kiss her cheek.

"I want you to understand something important," Grandma spoke softly so they had to pay attention. "I'm going for this exciting time of life, including this trip, because of your grandfather and parents. Not because they are gone, but because they are still here." She patted her heart. "I believe, with all my heart, that they want you to have good and happy lives, surrounded by those you love. And when there is a parting, like losing them, we will go on with happy lives as a tribute to them. Not only you youngsters..." She paused for affect. "...but me too. I want to go to Spain."

Applause and tears, amid smiles, came back to Grandma.

"Now, let's have dessert. I made a cholate cake and a coconut cake. Plenty of vanilla ice cream. Please, Matt and Charles, will you serve? Everything is ready in the kitchen, gentlemen. Silvia, the coffee, please. We await your pleasure."

Margaret put the sombrero back on Grandma's head. "You are so darn cute."

Chapter 20

Snow White Again

"Snow White," Lucille called up the stairs. "We cleaned the kitchen. Everybody is gone. Come down ... and watch your attitude." Lucille advised.

The very independent cat came down the stairs to prove she did not have an attitude. "I love peace and quiet. Don't say you don't, too."

"I love when they come, and I love when they go. Did you listen?" Grandma opened the conversation.

"Of course, every word."

"What's your opinion?"

"Me. Have an opinion?" Snow was ready to go back upstairs. "You could not have had a more wonderful day with the family. They all came around together to support you. That's what you wanted. That's what you needed. I'm happy for you." Snow turned and came back to Lucille. "Pick me up. I *do* have something else to tell you."

Lucille picked up her cat and settled her in her favorite way. "I watched from the window as they left. I saw Sarah and Tom holding hands. He even opened the car door for her. They were laughing and talking. Same with Pete and Sylvia."

"How about Sarah's black eyes. When you get that story from Margaret, I want to hear it." Snow laughed.

"I was not that surprised by Matt's friend Charlie. Were you?" Grandma asked

"Of course not. I had concern about him for a long time. He just couldn't get happy.

"What about my little speech at the end? I think I made a point with those kids."

"Yes, you did. I bet there were tears."

"The girls, for sure."

"Nice speech, but you missed a point. It could have been better."

"Sometimes you drive me crazy, Snow."

"Maybe . . . just maybe . . . you should have apologized. You haven't been keeping them clued into your mindset. Today, you did. Good job, ole girl," Snow went to Lucille's neck to pet her.

"I see. I'm partly at fault. You're right. I didn't insist they listen to me."

"For over a month, you've let them scoot out of this house without telling them what you planned to do. Never really told them your hopes and dreams much less your plan."

"I had doubts they would understand."

"An excuse," the attitude Lucile expected purred from her cat.

"I wanted them to grow up; give me a little room."

"Rightfully," Snow had to agree.

"I'm still thinking about telling them about the cancer." Finally, Lucille voiced what was troubling her.

"We've been all through that." Snow was getting the attitude Lucille had warned her against. "You know that I don't like rethinking things. Let's not rehash it. You decided not to tell, and I agreed. We are both tired. Leave it. Let's go to bed."

"Remind me, Smart Cat," Lucille needed to go over that hard decision again.

"Remember? How could you forget? You said it's all up to God. You wanted this trip before you knew about the cancer. Leave it with Him. *How, if,* or *when* you come back to A Street is not part of the decision. Besides, it's too late."

"Too late?"

"If you tell them now, you will have to cancel the trip. All the agreement and support you got tonight will evaporate. No Spain. No adventure. Just plain ole Grandma with a plain ole life." Snow reached her paw to Lucille's hand. "Don't go back."

"None of this is easy."

"Timing is everything, and today everything was right. Actually, the last wo years were beyond hard; this is easy. It was a perfect dinner."

Lucille appreciated Snow White's compliment and ruffled the fur on her head. "Yes. Today, everything got right." Lucille spoke with assurance. Snow White rolled over in her lap.

"They want to see you happy. If you are happy, you are not wallowing in grief. You're making your days interesting, making plans. Taking care of yourself. Living happy. They are happy if they know you are safe and happy. Period." Snow flicked her furry white tail in emphasis.

"It's not that simple," Lucille countered.

"Yes, it is," Snow White argued and hopped to the floor. "Just that simple." Snow headed to bed. "Enough looking back," she announced.

"Enough," Lucille agreed.

As Snow White meandered to the stairs, she shot back one more comment. "Good mentioning Irving, Patrick, and Joanne by name. It's therapeutic. Glad you did that."

Snow White gave Lucille a comforting thought to take to bed with her tired body.

Snow took the stairs like a white shadow. "Come on," she shouted back. "Last one to bed is a rotten egg!"

Chapter 21

Sonny Perkins

Grandma got out of bed the next morning, knowing exactly what she would do. She put on her gold shoes and the tee shirt with her self-portrait and fancy gold letters across the chest—*All that glitters is gold.* Margaret had the shirt made for her eightieth birthday. It put her in the right mood. She laid aside one large gold swirling pin that spelled Lucille and the matching earrings. Then she put them in the travel case with gobs and gobs of costume necklaces, bracelets, and earrings. Doc had told her not to bring her expensive jewelry but that was never her plan.

Lucille opened the empty top drawer of her dresser and put in little boxes each with the name of a granddaughter or a granddaughter-in-law. Slowly and systematically, the fine pieces of gold and precious stones were divided as equally as she could. She savored each piece, recalling where it had come from. There were chains of every length and gold necklaces with semi-precious stones, no doubt from QVC, a part of her wardrobe before Irving died. She loved them because they were from him, but they were not very imaginative. She handled the pieces that were given to her by Sarah, Regina, and Margaret as they went into their respective boxes. The pieces that came from the boys were returned to their wives' boxes. Then, she thought of Matt. He had selected excellent gifts over the years, but he did not have a wife. He had Charles. So, she labeled a box Matt/Charles and dropped in some fine stud earrings—each could wear one. That decision was good.

It was time for a cup of tea and a phone call. "Hi, Sonny. Is it your day off? I was wondering if you had some time. I could use some help."

She waited for Sonny Perkins to arrive and went about organizing letters for each grandchild. They were in alphabetical order on her desk. Lucille had thought long and hard about what she would write. Right now, the children seemed to understand her desire to go on this trip. She wonders if they really understand her need to fly away and do this thing that is so outside the box. Will they see that these last days or weeks or, maybe, months belong to her? They need to know that the death of Irving and their parents does not mean she is unable to decide for herself. It is true that the things children learn in a family begin when they are young. The lessons of wisdom and enlightenment come much later. Lucille had done all she could for them in their mid-lives. Maybe this determination to go will provide a good lesson for them when they reach the age of eighty-two. Lucille was dying, but she would not let the children hover over her and stifle her burning desire to live every day to the fullest. Their actions since Irving died prove that is exactly what they would do. Will they truly understand if the only thing returning from this trip will be her ashes? Lucille knows that when the time comes for their own demise, they will understand—fully. It never occurred to Lucille that this trip could be considered selfish; she had never done a selfish thing in her life.

The letters were placed in her desk drawer along with the key to her safe deposit box. Mark's name is on the card. It had taken her a long time to understand the living trust, but when she did, she could hardly wait to complete the paperwork and forget about it. So much for assets.

Lucille wanted Sonny to help clean out the house. "No one wants to think about dying, but there is some comfort in knowing I will be loved for these last chores," she said aloud as she stirred her tea. A knock interrupted her thoughts. "Hi, Sonny. How are things on the Salvation Army wagon? Collected any souls lately?"

"Grandma, that is an old joke."

"Well, I'm old and I tell old jokes."

"Ha!" he replied with a bear hug. "What's up? You wanted to see me on my day off?"

" I want to hire you for today."

"You don't have to hire me . . . think of all the meals you have fed Angie and me since I came here on my first day on the job. What do ya need? I'm ready to help. ... And, I like your shirt."

"I'm cleaning out, Sonny, before I go on my trip. I want to go room by room. I couldn't ask the grandchildren to help. They have too many opinions. You don't have any opinions with you today, do you?"

"Nope, left 'em all home."

"Good. Let's start in the front room. Here is what we need: black garbage bags, stick 'em notes, and pens. Who's the boss?"

"You are."

"I knew I had the right man for the job." She began by pointing to the things for the trash bag. Magazines, paperbacks, inexpensive knick-knacks.

"Whoa, Grandma. I think we need to bag some of these for the Salvation Army. We can sell 'em." The work continued. She pitched; he caught. Occasionally she paused to scribble a name on a stick 'em note and tucked it out of sight on something she wanted to keep and designate for a particular family member.

Sonny watched her pitch things like a person who never expected to live here again. He began to be uncomfortable in the effort. "Grandma, what's goin' on here? This room is beginning to look like a furniture display at the Laurel Furniture Store. There will be no sign of you in here when we finish."

"Come, Sonny, let's take a break and have some tea." She poured his tea over ice and put hers into a fine China cup as they sat at the table that he had never seen cleared before. She crossed her legs and fingers on the left hand as she lifted her cup and began to tell him the lie that she had prepared.

"Sonny, I'm not going to live here when I get back from my trip. I am moving to assisted living—Morningstar Place over on Contee Road. The children are going to help me make the move when I get back. I just want to make it easier for them." Lucille almost choked on the words, but she spit them out quickly and unwound all her twisted bones that made the lie okay.

Then she moved to put some cookies on the table to keep Sonny engaged in something besides her discomfort. He was eating cookies and drinking tea, but her words were causing him to have trouble swallowing. Thoughts were racing through his mind. He needed time to think about what he wanted to say. Maybe another cookie would help.

"Grandma ... I hate to tell you ... but, it seems I did bring one opinion with me after all."

Sonny was thinking he had no right to tell this dear eighty-two-year-old friend what to do. What does a boy only twenty-eight know about anything? Especially one who met Grandma months ago?

"Alright, Sonny." Grandma laughed. "Opinions are like bullets. They can go anywhere and sometimes they hit a target, but sometimes they miss. I'm listening."

"If I should come in here after you left and saw it striped and no sign of you, I would hate it. I can imagine how your grandchildren would feel."

She went down in her chair as if struck with one of the imaginary bullets. She threw her hand over her heart and feigned death. "Darn it, Sonny, you got me!" He was so right. It was wrong to take herself and every piece of Irving out of this house. Whatever the circumstances, the children should come to 206 A Street and find the spirit of the family here for them. She wanted to make things easier, but maybe she was wrong.

"That key is under the mat, right?" he asked

"Of course.

"It will be there while you are gone."

"Yes"

"You can bet Sarah, Mark, Pete or someone will come here and what are they going to think with everything stripped bare. If we go on with this, I will never come in again. Not even for a drink of water when I'm passing down Main Street."

They went back to the living room and replaced things that were sentimental. Books and cheap pictures were put back. Irving's old afghan was tossed across the sofa. She left the sticky notes. When they moved to the other rooms, only trash was bagged up. It took a lot less time. Sonny was gone before lunch. Lucille had plenty of time to continue putting sticky notes on things.

Her last night in the house was better because of Sonny. She would have hated it too if all the personality was gone: signs of her and Irving; family snapshots tucked in picture frames; half-filled perfumes, gifts from them; anniversary and birthday cards; souvenirs collected on trips; magnets on the refrigerator. She knew Sonny was right. Suppose she did live to return to A Street. Lucille Cotton would hate to come into this house reduced to a shell of her life as much as her grandchildren would.

A sticky note was put on the back of her mirror in the hallway. "Sonny Perkins." She took her pen and wrote one more letter to Sonny Perkins, driver for the Salvation Army. She thanked him for his help and reminded her that not all wisdom requires eight decades.

She put the letters she wrote to Sarah, Jim, Matt, Pete, John, Mark, Margaret, and Regina in a drawer. She did not want them found and read before the desk was cleaned out.

Her grandchildren would figure things out just as Sonny did, and they would move confidently through their futures. Possibly, she would see it happen from an angel's perch.

"God only knows," she spoke to Snow White as she climbed the stairs.

Chapter 22

The Finest Cotton

On departure day, Doc picked Lucille up at 11:30 in a limousine.

"My, you look wonderful, Lucy." She took the hand he offered and slid into the seat, ready to begin her big adventure.

She decided to talk to Doc about the only shred of apprehension she had about their trip. "Doc, do you think I am being selfish going away on this trip now? I doubt I will ever see 206 A Street or my family again."

Doc thought carefully before answering this dear friend. He was the one who should be able to give her the best answer. He knew her cancer, and in the final stages, she would be able to function unless she was incapacitated by treatments. She made the choice to live until she dies. It was the most unselfish act he could imagine. It gave him courage with his own health issues. Either way, he should have more time than she, and that was his prayer. He did not have a crystal ball, but he had a gut feeling that he could and would be able to care for her. Furthermore, he had a divine feeling that going on this trip together was the right thing for both of them.

"Lucy, you are not selfish to go. I understand your doubts, but you don't know you will *not* return. No one knows. If you live to the fullest and strive to be happy in all the time left, you will be an inspiration to the generation of Cottons waiting for us right now at the Hilton Atrium."

"Help me, Doc. Help me avoid those terrible bedside visuals and sad faces on my grandchildren. Take me to bright days and new places so they will always picture me as I am today."

"Done." *And, what a beautiful picture it is,* he thought.

Lucille spent all last week getting ready for this day. On Tuesday, she went to the New Image Salon. It was time to tone down her curls.

"Amanda, soften the color to blend with white roots. Maybe a platinum color. More natural."

"I thought you like red, Ms. Lucille."

"Oh, I did. I did, but now I'm ready for a change."

She left the salon without Bernadette Peters' curl but sophisticated curls—far, far from mousy grey.

Lucille had to select the right clothes for her departure day. The children would gather for lunch at the Hilton's Atrium before she and Doc took the limo to Baltimore/Washington International Airport. It was a great idea. He knew the steady stream of good-by-sayers through the little house on A Street could possibly interfere with her preparations to leave. Doc called them and extended the invitation to the luxurious hotel restaurant on Airport Drive. A leisurely lunch. The flight was at 7:15. This was his first plan to make this trip perfect; he had many more. After the family dinner last week, he could see how tired she was, and he did not want to start this trip with the little lady worn out. Her departure had to be special; it could possibly be more than just goodbye for a couple of months, so he made a list of details before departing. The top one was making sure she had plenty of time to say farewell to the children. He planned for her personal well-being and her health needs. There were medicines with special permits and advanced contacts with medical associations in Spain in case he needed some help. He planned for his own needs too. There were letters to write: two for his nieces and one for Mark. They would deserve an explanation that included his medical expertise.

Lucille looked wonderful. The sparkle in her eye and the lift in her step were back. She decided to be Betty Davis sailing way on an ocean liner in 1947, even though in reality, it would be a 747 in 1987. Her new little hat was perched on top of her white, shiny curls that swept around it like silver ringlets. Her three-piece travel ensemble was art deco with a broad collar, buttons swirling up the jacket, one large sweeping silver pin, and a straight skirt. Today's color was a dark rich sapphire, and her hat and shoes matched perfectly. Gloria in Hecht's hosiery department had even found a pair of pantyhose that had a slight tinge of blue. When she was all adorned, she looked in the mirror and smiled back at herself. It was almost perfect. "What a pity," she said to her mirror image, "this hat needs a big feather, and I don't have time to get one." Her pin on the broad collar spelled her name. Irving had it made for her on their 50th Anniversary, and it deserved to go with her.

♔ ♔ ♔

The children were seated when they entered the restaurant, and applause seemed appropriate. Grandma took a sweeping bow as Doc led her to her seat.

"Is she someone important?" The head waiter asked his comrade.

"Must be," he replied as he quickly began pouring ice water into the goblets.

"I notice only you grandchildren are here. Where is everyone else?" Grandma asked as she counted heads.

We decided at this table nine is enough," said John. "Including Doc, of course."

"Mark, our blessing, and we can get on with the meal."

"Our Heavenly Father, . . .

"Wait, wait," came a voice from across the restaurant. "Make room for the prodigal."

It was Regina! Excitement disrupted the entire restaurant as she flew between tables, knocking against people with her carry-on and a huge tote, which made unusual clanging noises each time she banged a chair. "Excuse me . . . excuse me." The waiter, sure that she was important, rushed to help her join the gathering in the center of the room.

Regina. a colorful tornado, swept across the room, dressed in African animal print attire with earth colors lit by the sun filtering through the atrium. Her golden curls were topped with a pillbox hat of the same African print. Her attire brought a herd of antelopes and a pride of jungle cats to this hotel oasis. There was no doubt that she belonged to the lady who shared the limelight.

"*Aburagiri,* everyone. I made it! Six hours by jeep across the desert and twenty-one hours flying from Morocco—three air-lines." She sat down and with a sigh, looked around the table at the family she missed so much. "I was determined since I talked to you last week, Grandma. I had to be here so I wouldn't miss launching you on the adventure of your life. And, I wanted the chance to say, *you go girl!*"

Grandma was the first to give a big bear hug before Regina moved around the table, where each sibling gave her the attention of a long-lost love. While this was going on, the waiter had discreetly moved place settings until there was room for one more at the big round table.

"Let's get the blessing done." John wanted to move things along. Harri was waiting for him with blessings of her own.

"Our Heavenly Father, Thank you for bringing Regina safely to us. Please bless this family and especially Grandma who is prepared to leave us for a very important journey. Keep her safe; keep her happy and keep her close to You. Bless Doc as he accompanies her. We ask for your blessing for each family member as we go on with our lives while Grandma is gone. We ask your guidance so we can always be close to each other and to You. Thank you for this meal; it is a reminder that all good things come from You. Amen."

"I think you are getting better, Mark."

"Thanks, Grandma."

"Are we going to have a Cotton pickin' today?" Asked Regina.

"We sure are. Right after we order our food and have the toast. Would not want to miss a Cotton pickin' when we have Regina here to take her knocks." Matt smiled at his beloved sister.

"Doc, I have ordered wine and let's get everyone loosened

up a bit!" Pete had to take charge of something.

The wine did its magic as everyone relaxed. The waiter could not figure out who the little lady with platinum curls was but concluded that the lady in African dress was an actress that he had seen in a movie with Robert Redford, although he could not recall her name. He kept the wine coming and the service prompt.

While everyone was reading the menu and making selections, Grandma looked around the table, assessing and storing the mental picture of each grandchild for times when she needed the memory. *Regina was most like me, but not in stature. She had Irving's height but my spirit. Her courage came early, she claimed the world, and she could bring it home to us whenever she had time. Her wisdom was as strong as an elephant and as comfortable as a breeze.* It seemed to Grandma that Regina's brothers and sisters admired her adventurous nature, but it did not relate to their everyday lives.

Pete and Matt, dressed alike in khaki pants and navy-blue blazers, ordered Merlot in unison. They were not sitting side by side, thus avoiding a double vision. Each in his own way special, and both unaware of the fun they add to the family. Grandma was sure they were finally looking at their siblings as equals, balancing brains with common sense.

Jim got the waiter's attention to take the wine glass away and bring Jack Daniels as his special guest at this party. "I don't drink adult cool-aid. I think wine is the biggest hoax played on the public. It is the only drink that needs propaganda to convince people it is good. Tennessee should be commended for sharing Jack with the rest of the world . . . but I will concede that Kentucky knows a thing or two about filling a glass. These days, I only have one ounce, but it's a good one." Jim will always challenge his siblings with self-questioning—*am I doing this because everyone else is or because I want to?*

Margaret was the family smile. Looking almost ageless, she was dressed in the latest fashion that many young matrons wished they could wear. Her hair and makeup were perfect, and she had the look that she could shake her hair down and run through the grass if there was a moment's pleasure in it.

John was Irving. *How come I never saw that before?* Grandma thought as she watched him enjoying all this commotion, loving all the characters but a little set apart. He was the constant, handsome rock in this group. *Irving all over.* When she caught his eye, he responded by walking to where she could kiss him. It was hardly noticed around the table. Lucille took a deep breath and bid *Irving* another farewell. After almost two years she was surprised when grief swept over her at unsuspecting times.

Sarah was assessing, looking around the table at each one. Her gaze stopped at Grandma and Doc. The question would have to be asked, and she was glad she was seated next to her grandmother to be less conspicuous in the asking. She waited until they were busy ordering. "Grandma . . . umm . . . I was wond . . .

"For heaven's sake, Sarah, spit it out."

"Is Doc going with you because you need a doctor on the trip? Are you and Doc in . . . love?"

Grandma wanted to choose her words well and not lie to her wonderful granddaughter. Grandma loved Sarah most of all because she loved so hard and had more demons, more doubts and less optimism than all the rest put together. Sarah was just too responsible! She reached over and took Sarah's two hands in hers, gave her granddaughter a big smile and answered.

"My dear child. We are eighty-two and eighty-four years old. We don't know how long our health will allow us to do things like this trip, but we are willing to risk the chance that one or both of our clocks may run out while we are away. We are asking you and your brothers and sisters to take that risk with us. I admit to you that it is a great comfort to have him with me. You know he is a dear old friend; being a doctor is a plus. It should make you feel better about our trip, not add apprehensive. I don't want to see him naked, and he surely isn't going to see me without my full regalia. There is no way to turn back the hands of time on our trip, and we do not want to turn them back

"Grandma, you look so happy."

"Dear, I am happy; keep that thought."

She touched Sarah's forehead with her own and they were engulfed in giggles. As Sarah said, "If I ever grow up, I want to be just like you."

"Lucy, you had better look at the menu; decide what you want." Doc was moving things along.

"I know exactly what I want! A Maryland lunch—Cobb salad, named for that wonderful island in the bay. Rockfish that slept last night in the Chesapeake Bay; stuffed with blue claw crab—also from the bay and French-fried potatoes sprinkled with Old Bay seasoning. Is that the perfect lunch for today—or what?"

"Almost perfect, Grandma, if you include a tall slice of Smith Island Cake for desert. Yellow with dark chocolate icing," Matt added.

The meal was lively, the talk engaging, and the fun infectious. They took their time eating, drinking, and talking. The clock was moving past three, the other patrons had reluctantly left them for the real world outside when, with a tap on the water goblet, Margaret demanded attention.

"I'll start the Cotton pickin'. Just want you to know I am going to Spain with Freddy as soon as the race season is over. Grandma, you got the red curls before I could, but I got *Fredrico!* We will be in Spain this winter. Grandma and Doc, have a wonderful time."

Jim took his turn. "I am working out! I am healthy and loving it. I promised Grandma to eat and drink in moderation, and she even got me to promise to drive in moderation. I'm working on that." He started to sit down but rose again. "Wait, wait, I have another piece of cotton. I almost forgot, Marge and I are making plans to go over the big pond to meet with Grandma in Spain . . . or Portugal if they extend their trip." That brought a round of applause.

Will and Pete came out of their seats together, and everyone laughed.

"You first," said Pete

"No, you first," replied Matt as everyone around the table rolled their eyes at this very old scenario. Pete insisted because he loved rebuttal.

"Charles and I are being married in a civil ceremony in California next month. We will send pictures, and we expect a great party when we return. Our union will not be sanctioned in Maryland, but we are hoping it is in this family where it counts." Grandma blew him a kiss.

Pete took his turn. "I'm not running away with anyone, not even running to anything. Sylvia and I are happy where we are—playing a little golf." This brought a laugh. "Alright, maybe a lot of golf and volunteering at the soup kitchen downtown. We are on Mark's Team-Jesus. And we are putting in a swimming pool this summer so I hope you will all come, with your significant others, and spend lots of time with us around it. Thanks, Grandma for jerking my chain when I needed it. We love you."

"I have an announcement, too." started John. "Fill the glasses; this requires a toast." Glasses were refilled and ready. "Harri and I have developed a line of golf shirts called Cotton Patch, and six PGA pros are already wearing them. You know Harri is quite a seamstress." He took off his sport coat and showed the cream-colored shirt with a Cotton Bowl and a tiny Maryland flag embroidered over the left breast. "She designed the logo, and here is the secret that makes the shirt special. See these little extra insets, here and here?" He demonstrated by pointing to the sleeve and collar. "I saw the golfers constantly pulling the shoulder of their shirts before hitting a ball. They pulled right below the collar. I've solved that, and they could always use ease in the sleeves. It is 100% cotton, the finest cotton, and woven for extra breath. All I had to do was get them to try the prototype. They will be going out retail by Christmas."

"Here. Here. John." The drinks were raised, and applause followed.

"I'll take three," said Pete and Matt in unison.

"I'd like a couple too . . . but not until I know how much they cost, and what's the family discount," was Jim's comment. "I call on Mark. Since he isn't the last one, he will have to say something besides a prayer!"

Mark was very short in his remarks. "I am going to be a chaplain of the streets—ministering at the food kitchen and hoping my service helps and brings people to God. No big church, no budget, no organization. Just a cross on my lapel and God in my heart."

"Mark," said Grandma with love in her voice, "that is wonderful, and remember, if any of those souls need to come in out of the rain, the key is under the mat at 206 A Street."

"It's Regina's turn! I call on our sister of the world! Regina, it is time for you to get in the Cotton patch; it's been a long time." Mark turned the spotlight on his sister.

Regina rose very slowly and looked around as if she were surveying the Serengeti. She straightened her dress and hat while looking for her words. It was obvious she had been more engrossed in what her brothers and sisters were saying than in composing her thoughts.

"There is so much I want to say. I have come from a place where the future is very fragile, and I learned that, in fact, that is true everywhere. Here, in the comfort of our family and homes, we deny that truth. It is easy with security and comfort to forget. Forever is never a promise. The future is really not a part of our lives. It is so wonderful being here with Grandma and you on this occasion. We have this happy presence."

There was a danger that Regina's serious words would bring the party down. However, that was not going to happen with this bright spirit.

"So. Like the tribes of Tanzania, I would like to celebrate today and not worry about the future." With that said, Regina kicked off her shoes and reached into her big tote bag to pull out flat drums for her brothers and tambourines for her sisters. Around the table she danced, lifting the long colorful dress to show her tanned ankles and bare feet doing the most wonderful steps and twirls. The spirit and sound grew as she set the tempo with her motions. Margaret and Sarah joined Regina. They were tapping the tambourines and moving as if they had been dancing amid huts and dust all their lives. John, Jim, Matt, Pete, and Mark stayed in their seatd and joined the beat on their drums. The nearly empty restaurant atrium was suddenly transformed into Africa. Regina was the star the waiter believed she was. Grandma rose and began to follow around the table. Just enough wine and Jack had been consumed to keep everyone uninhibited. Doc held his seat until the dancers stopped. Then he took Grandma's hand and led her to her place. Mark, John, Jim, Pete, and Matt finished with grand percussion flurries on their drums.

Regina came to Grandma. "I'm going to see you in Barcelona. Doc gave me your itinerary. Can't wait."

"While you are here, stay at the house. The key is under the mat. How long are you staying?"

"A few days, a week at most."

"Perfect. Snow White can stay with you at the house. Charles and Matt have agreed to give her a home and take care of her. But she will enjoy some extra time at A Street and being with you. You are one of her favorites."

John rose. He had some business to tend to, as always. "Here's to the Cotton family. Here's to Mom and Dad and Grandpa; they are always with us. We could never thank Grandma enough for holding this family together during these difficult years. Here's to Grandma From this spot to anyplace, from this time to always—Grandma, you are the finest Cotton!"

Grandma could not be happier or more confident that this band of renegades was a family. A family pulled together by her shenanigans and held together with a genuine love that was maturing before her happy eyes. She was positive, in the future, there would be many happy gatherings like this during every season and for every reason under the sun. She would not be with them, but that did not matter. Not one little bit, not one little cotton ball.

"Hear! Hear! Grandma. Lucille Cotton. The finest Cotton." They proclaimed

Chapter 23

Snow White Again, Again

Regina went to the house on A Street and found the key under the mat, just as Grandma said. She shook her head at the security system the mat provided. After opening the door, she replaced the key just as Grandma said.

"Snow White," Regina called. "Snow White. Where is that cat?" she spoke to the seemingly empty house. "I know you are here and expecting Matt and Charles," Regina continued to talk as she passed through the living room to the kitchen. "Snow White, come see me," she invited. "It's Regina," she informed.

Snow White quickly descended the stairs and ran to Regina's feet inviting her to pick her up with an unusual display of affection. She leaned into the hug that Regina offered.

"Grandma has had a great send-off. All is quiet in the family. I'm staying here for a few days. Matt will come for you after I leave."

"Regina!" Snow White exclaimed. "I didn't expect to see you

and have someone to talk to. I am so happy. Let's sit in the kitchen. Make tea. I have so much to tell you." Snow's voice was animated as she greeted one of her favorite Cottons. As they walked to the kitchen, Snow continued. "Living with Matt and Charles will be fine. No kids or dogs, and I think I can talk to Charles. I hope I can talk to Charles. But first, tell me about Africa."

The End

Epilogue

Sarah tried not to be a donkey's ass, but lifelong habits do not change easily. She still thought she knew what was best for everyone and often told her brothers and sisters what they should think and what they should do. The subtle change was her acceptance of their reluctance to fall in step. Sarah decided to lighten-up and listened to Tom more often. She also planned an aroma bath every Wednesday evening when Tom worked late. No grandchildren. Some wine. Tom thought that was one of Sarah's best ideas. Working late on Wednesday took on new meaning when he came home to a relaxed, mellow, good smelling, happy wife.

John continued to boycott family meetings. It had to be something very important for him to make the effort. It wasn't necessarily that he didn't want to gather with the family. It was because he always seemed to have something better to do with his bride.

Mark became the family compass. He gently took on the responsibility of caring for everyone without making requirements. Mark stepped into Grandma's shoes. He didn't realize it and his siblings barely defined it. Mark was just always there.

He knew his siblings were impatient and short on attention when he insisted on prayers. That was fine. Mark included their inattentiveness in his prayers.

Pete stopped trying to be more than his brother. He embraced his twin and viewed Matt as his own person. They stopped looking for their own reflection in each other.

Pete and Sylvia put in the pool and made their home the summer gathering place for the family. It was new. It was fun. Being together, splashing in the pool, and eating overcooked hamburgers from the grill, helped everyone enjoy the summer without Grandma. Matt and Charles joined the fun unless they were traveling.

Charles tried to tell Matt that Snow White spoke to him. He tried to tell him twice. Then on advice from Snow, Charles decided to *just let it go.*

Jim continued to drive too fast. He bought a fully restore 1967 Corvette. When Marge asked him why he bought another Corvette, Jim replied, "why not."

Margaret lived the free life she enjoyed. She became enamored by thoroughbred horses and the excitement of racetracks. She was usually accompanied by a handsome Spaniard.

Regina went back to Africa.

Late that summer when hints of fall filled the air, Sarah held the door as her sister and brothers filed into her kitchen. They came in and began talking at once. Matt, Pete, Margaret, Mark, Jim, and John. Everyone came except the ever-absent, Regina.

"Snacks on the counter. Help yourselves to drinks." Sarah sat at the kitchen table with Jim and Mark. Her notes and a telegram were in front of her. Margaret and John sat at the counter on stools. Pete and Matt chose to stand. Sarah had three kinds of fresh cookies on the table plus coffee and iced tea. Mark picked a seat closest to the cookies.

Sarah looked up at her brothers and sister and said, "This meeting is about Grandma..."

The End Again